ELIZABETH TAYLOR

(1912–1975) was born Elizabeth Coles in Reading, Berkshire. The daughter of an insurance inspector, she was educated at the Abbey School, Reading, and after leaving school worked as a governess and, later, in a library. At the age of twenty-four she married John William Kendall Taylor, a businessman, with whom she had a son and a daughter. She lived much of her married life in the village of Penn in Buckinghamshire.

Elizabeth Taylor wrote her first novel, *At Mrs Lippincote's* (1945), during the war while her husband was in the Royal Air Force. This was followed by *Palladian* (1946), *A View of the Harbour* (1947), *A Wreath of Roses* (1949), *A Game of Hide and Seek* (1951), *The Sleeping Beauty* (1953), *Angel* (1957), *In a Summer Season* (1961), *The Soul of Kindness* (1964), *The Wedding Group* (1968), *Mrs Palfrey at the Claremont* (1971) and *Blaming*, published posthumously in 1976. She has also published four volumes of short stories: *Hester Lilly and Other Stories* (1954), *The Blush and Other Stories* (1958), *A Dedicated Man and Other Stories* (1965) and *The Devastating Boys* (1972). Elizabeth Taylor has written a book for children, *Mossy Trotter* (1967); her short stories have been published in the *New Yorker*, *Harper's Bazaar*, *Harper's* magazine, *Vogue* and the *Saturday Evening Post*, and she is included in *Penguin Modern Stories 6*.

Critically Elizabeth Taylor is one of the most acclaimed British novelists of this century, and in 1984 *Angel* was selected as one of the Book Marketing Council's "Best Novels of Our Time". Virago publishes all of her sixteen works of fiction.

VIRAGO
MODERN
CLASSIC

NUMBER
392

Elizabeth Taylor

A WREATH
OF ROSES

Introduction by Candia McWilliam

"So terrible was life that I held up shade
after shade. Look at life through this, look
at life through that; let there be rose leaves,
let there be vine leaves—I covered the whole
street, Oxford Street, Piccadilly Circus, with
the blaze and ripple of my mind, with vine
leaves and rose leaves."

VIRGINIA WOOLF: THE WAVES

To
Maud Geddes

Published by VIRAGO PRESS Limited January 1994
20–23 Mandela Street, Camden Town, London NW1 0HQ

First published in Great Britain by Peter Davies Ltd. 1949
Copyright © Elizabeth Taylor 1949
Introduction copyright © Candia McWilliam 1993

A CIP catalogue record for this book is available from the British Library

Printed and bound in Great Britain by
Cox & Wyman Ltd, Reading, Berkshire

INTRODUCTION

Frances, the painter/mentor who presides over *A Wreath of Roses*, "would rather be praised for her crab apple jelly than her painting". Susannah Clapp has observed that in Frances, Elizabeth Taylor offered something of herself – also an artist who cultivated a bourgeois, anti-Bohemian life, as recommended by Flaubert.

Frances has tired of the scenes she used to paint, of fruit and flowers and young women in rooms. She rebukes herself: "I committed a grave sin against the suffering of the world by ignoring it, by tempting others with charm and nostalgia until they ignored it too." Her latest paintings, though, show "the white bones of the earth and dark figures scurrying against a violet sky."

In the view of Morland, an old admirer of Frances's work, it is not the more overtly daring, newer paintings, but the earlier ones that surprise, that "turned life a little under his very eyes." Both Frances's misgivings about the scale and manner of her art and Morland's conviction that life is better shown in vivid fragments, are given proper weight; the argument, or rather, temperamental confrontation, doesn't distort the surface of the novel. No one steps out of the frame to engage in post-modern debate, as they might if they were actually alive, after the subsequent decades of noisy traducement of novels written by middle-class Englishwomen. The process by which a thoughtful socialist like Elizabeth Taylor came to be so categorised, evidences an irony about literary fashion as little noticed as that by which the thoroughly European Anita Brookner allegedly represents a limited Englishness in contemporary fiction. The reputations of such writers have a way of surviving their detractors through the private but persistent devotion of their readers. The kind of non-reader who is convinced that Elizabeth Taylor is a toothless quietest painting in pastel should try trimming the whiskers and manicuring the paws of pumas.

The novels of Elizabeth Taylor do, it is true, often have quiet, painterly titles. She wrote of herself, in the *New York Herald Tribune* Books Section in 1953: "I am always disconcerted when I am asked for my life story, for nothing sensational, thank heavens, has ever happened. I dislike much travel or change of environment, and prefer the days (each with its own domestic flavour) to come round almost the same, week after week, Only in such circumstances can I find time or peace in which to write. I also very much like reading books in which practically nothing ever happens." This masterpiece of grisaille goes against the hectic manner in which writers are currently presented. It rings true in a way to which, if we neglect the work of such writers, we shall forget how to respond, finding ourselves left with a hunger for certain kinds of subtlety and precision which we will cease to seek in books, coming eventually, perhaps, to cease noting them in our own lives.

As I write, almost twenty years after her death, I have been sent a "distinguished" new study of the English novel since the Second World War which contains not one mention of Elizabeth Taylor. Yet she is, morally and artistically, one of the most *certain* artists of the period. Perhaps the distinguished critic is deceived by Taylor's sex, class, and quiet country life in Penn, Buckinghamshire, where she said that she enjoyed observing and thinking about the weather. It should be added though, that Taylor would certainly have preferred this benign neglect to the attentions of some grimly modish French critic, who would note the siginifcance of the name of the village, or the preponderant use in today's millenialist novels of weather as a metaphor for chaos and doom.

The paradoxical conformism of our times seems dispiritingly unable to assimilate this nicely-spoken egalitarian, and unprepared to see that although she does write about, for example, domestic servants, she does so not solely to draft their labour in a polemic of her making, but to show them as individuals, and individuals often badly used. Similarly, considering the quiet, light-endowing, scene-making that is her greatest skill, the hasty or the deafened trample over the *idea* of her prose; over the prose itself it is less easy to trample. The reader is brought up short by its clarity, mercy, and ease with natural beauty and human malice alike.

A Wreath of Roses confronts things constant – friendship, children, work, domestic life – with things melodramatic – suicide, betrayal, war, sudden lust. In a sense the first category of things is the preserve of the women in the book and the second of the book's pivotal male character; a man of mystery who is putting up at an hotel in the small town where unmarried Camilla and sweet Liz and her baby son are making their annual visit to Frances, who is Liz's old governess.

Frances's personal style is tart and straight; she has managed to put her life into those of others and to pursue her life as an artist – an almost impossible combination, though one which Elizabeth Taylor also achieved. Camilla is a teacher who has been raised among brothers and the booming voices and important pursuits of men, to which, she has gathered, her own are inferior. She is intelligent, almost still beautiful, and old to be a virgin. Liz is married to a vicar who enjoys multiple flirtations with his lady parishioners. Her huband and her son make her at once somehow inferior (for conforming with biology) and an object of envy to Camilla. The women all profoundly love one another – which stops neither criticism nor some disloyalty. The pleasures of female friendship recur in Elizabeth Taylor's work, less breathless than love between men and women always, and safer too.

More solid and less important than the desperate man at the heart of the book is the admirer of Frances's work, Morland. He shows up both Arthur, Liz's fustian husband and the glamorous, inadvisable mystery man, in a way that women do not care to have their menfolk shown up. He is less under illusion's spell than Camilla and Liz, rather more so than Frances. Yet illusion is a comfort necessary to the younger women, and it will eventually help them to continue, after the crises related in the novel, with their lives.

Frances is preoccupied, but unillsuioned: "My work is my love", she thinks, "My consolation and refuge. In the midst of other people, against the thought of death, of war, I turn the secret page in my own mind, knowing that though I seem to have less than others, in reality I have more than ever I bargained for."

She goes out to pick tomatoes, with their "lovely sharp fragrance", into the new day. "It was a pearly morning: the sky, which had been cloudless for days, had flocks of little clouds across it, like a sky painted on a ceiling; but still the sun dazzled, the red ants like garnets ran in the parched grass".

She knows her life is coming to its end. The large disobliging dog, Hotchkiss, she has acquired as a companion, lumbers, dribbling, after her, an imposition upon Liz and Camilla in a physical way Frances herself never has been and never will be. Frances has found a way of loving that is lighter and more free than family love: "And the great happiness I have over Liz, bringing her up and loving her, could not have been more intense if I had been her own mother." She blames herself for her self-sufficiency, but it has enabled her to work, and it has been her only sin.

For Camilla, such intensity of focus is briefly called up by her sudden passion for the man whom she meets, over a suicide, at the book's inception, despising him at once for his looks: "All of his clothes and his bearing depicting a kind of man who could never have any part in her life, whose existence could not touch hers, which was thoughtful rather than active and counted its values in a different way. All this they knew at a glance. That they should trouble to explore one another further was explained by the empty afternoon, the feeling that time was being paid out too slowly to bring the train they awaited."

Elizabeth Taylor has the gift of contorting time with her words, pulling it out thin and long or exploding it with events. It is a torsion that intensifies the pleasure of reading her novels. All too soon in *A Wreath of Roses*, time is being paid out at speed, and Camilla is looking into the mirror of a pub: "[She] felt as if the day had been a dream, that she would come out of it soon, lifting fold after fold of muffling web; for this could not be real – meeting Liz again after eleven months and finding herself so alienated from her that she could show off to her about a man. 'And *this* sort of man!' she thought, glancing at him through the mirror. Their eyes met. Alone in the looking-glass they seemed. They watched, with a steady fascination, as if those two other selves would commit some action independently of them; would among the reflected bottles; the ferns, glasses, turn to one another in the closest intimacy, make some violent impact upon one another which could not be made in actuality.

"Camilla lowered her eyes, stood very still, as if now the mirror were going to crack in two. The room tipped and lurched, people's faces ran together, their voices slipping and painful in her ears. One brush of his sleeve gainst her arm and the bar, she felt, would burst into flame."

The transforming power of desire and its awful damage return in the novels and stories of Elizabeth Taylor, including her masterpiece *Angel*, in which the object of Angel's passion is tired out by it. In *A Wreath of Roses*, this emotion turns around on itself, so that there is a shocking circularity to the novel, which painfully sets the thorny ending of this story deep in the throat of its beginning, making a wreath of its incidental full-flowering beauties that open their complicated faces to the reader, and show human self-deception and aspiration in all their layers, down to the heart.

Candia McWilliam, Oxford, 1993

CHAPTER ONE

AFTERNOONS seem unending on branch-line stations in England in summer time. The spiked shelter prints an unmoving shadow on the platform, geraniums blaze, whitewashed stones assault the eye. Such trains as come only add to the air of fantasy, to the idea of the scene being symbolic, or encountered at one level while suggesting another even more alienating.

Once the train which had left them on the platform had drawn out, the man and woman trod separately up and down, read time-tables in turn, were conscious of one another in the way that strangers are, when thrown together without a reason for conversation. A word or two would have put them at ease, but there were no words to say. The heat of the afternoon was beyond comment and could not draw them together as hail-stones might have done. They had nothing to do, but to walk up and down or sit for a moment on the blistering-hot, slatted seat. In any case, they would not naturally have made efforts to exchange words, since he was a man of conventional good-looks of the kind that she, Camilla, believed she despised—the empty grey eyes with their thick lashes, the waving hair, the weak, square chin, rather cleft; all of his clothes and his bearing depicting a kind of man who could never have any part in her life, whose existence could not touch hers, which was thoughtful rather than active and counted its values in a different way. All this they knew at a glance. That they should trouble to explore one another further was explained by the empty afternoon, the feeling that time was being paid out too slowly to bring the train they awaited.

She turned back her cuff to see the time, patted her yawning mouth with her fist. Heedless of her appearance, he thought; and the little beauty she possessed could be in the eyes of only a few beholders, so much was it left to fend for itself. She made no concessions, beyond neatness, in order to arrest or distract and ordinarily he would not have glanced at her again.

At last she sat down on a seat and opened a book. This seemed to leave him alone on the platform under the blazing sun. Shut up in a little office, the station-master whistled through his teeth. The sound came out of the window, and sometimes the scraping on the wooden floor when he moved his chair. Out on the white country road, a horse and cart waited and the horse crunched the gravel, worn out with the flies, the heat. Then, with a collapsing sound, the signal dropped.

The woman looked up and then at the clock and then back at her book. When another man walked on to the platform, she sat with her finger on a word, watching him going up the steps of the footbridge and could hear the hollow sound of his boots on the wooden boards.

The train's white plume came slowly towards them; but neither stirred, for this was a through train, against which they rather braced themselves, watching the shabby man idling his afternoon away on the bridge like a child looking at trains.

The station-master came out of his office and stood in the doorway. The three of them were quite still in the shimmering heat, the plume of smoke nodding towards them, the noise of the train suddenly coming as it rounded a bend, suddenly sucking them up in its confusion and panic. All at once, the man on the footbridge swung himself up on the parapet and, just as Camilla was putting out her arms in a ridiculous gesture as if to stop him, he clumsily jumped, a sprawling jump, an ill-devised death, since he fell wide of the express train.

This happening broke the afternoon in two. The feeling of eternity had vanished. What had been timeless and silent became chaotic and disorganised, with feet running along the echoing boards, voices staccato, and the afternoon darkening with the vultures of disaster, who felt the presence of death and arrived from the village to savour it and to explain the happening to one another.

But before an ambulance could come, he died, quietly, his back broken. He lay in a little patch of shade outside the station-master's office, beyond which they had not managed to carry him. The vultures gathered close, to stand between him and the afternoon. He died at their feet and the station-master covered him with an old coat so that only his boots, beautifully polished, were left to their mercy.

Camilla walked to the far end of the platform, and when her train drew in at last, she sat down in an empty compartment and closed her eyes.

And now the afternoon had taken one step towards evening. She could sense herself going towards it, the shadows drawn out across lawns and pavements, elm trees full of a blue darkness, gnats golden in the air.

To her shocked mind, it seemed that the death she had witnessed was not to be so easily left behind as the train moved forward; but that it would go along with her. She experienced a moment of fear and recoil, introduced by that happening, but related to the future as well.

Just as the train began to move, the young man who had awaited it for so long, wrenched at the door and jumped into the carriage, breathing desperately, as if he had run a long way and at great pace. Unsteadily he threw his suitcase along the seat, and sat down opposite Camilla, who at once (for such was her instinct) turned to contemplate the sweltering fields, the drowsy, wooded horizon.

"Upsetting!" he said suddenly, his eyes upon her as he wiped his palms on a silk handkerchief.

"Something more than upsetting," she rebuked him, and turned again to the unrolling landscape, but he saw tears under her lashes as she looked away.

4

"I wonder why . . . ?" he went on, determined now to make those tears fall if he could. As though she realised this, she made a great effort to steady herself and managed at last to answer in a callous, off-hand manner: "If he couldn't manage his death better than that, the difficulties of living were obviously beyond him."

'A schoolmistress,' he decided.

"That chorus!" she cried, shaken with rage.

"Chorus?"

"The ones who gathered from nowhere and stood watching and explaining."

"Oh, I see."

"Their tongues flicking up and down like snakes' tongues."

He looked at her curiously.

"Perhaps you can't blame them," he suggested.

"*You* blamed them. You walked away . . . at least, I missed you . . ."

She hesitated and looked up and he saw that her eyes were brilliantly blue.

"What station is this?" she asked, leaning to the window as the train slowed past a signal-box.

"Broad Oak," he read. There were the words suddenly, very white on black, and the same deserted platform, the geraniums; as if they had completed a circle. Only the shadows were shifting and drawing themselves out.

She leant back again.

"How far are you going?"

"To Abingford."

5

"For a holiday?"

"Yes."

"And staying at the Red Lion, I expect?"

"The Red Lion?" she asked, puzzled.

"It is the Red Lion, isn't it? The big one in the High Street?"

"The High Street?"

"The main street, the wide one," he said, as if with impatience.

"You must mean Market Street."

"Well, isn't the Red Lion there?"

"No. The one with the porch and the stuccoed pillars is The Bear. The only other is in Market Square, opposite the station, a place with shutters and a cobbled yard at the side." She closed her eyes for a moment, trying to remember. "The Griffin," she said suddenly. "Yes, the Griffin."

"Oh, I've forgotten. A sentimental journey, this. I was a boy when I was here last. Now I've come back for some peace; to write a book, in fact."

She was surprised. Her imagination refused this idea, refused the idea of him *reading* a book even. A man, she would have thought him, bound by cold, impersonal interests and dull, objective conversation—sport, and newspapers, and the price of cars.

"What kind of book?" she enquired.

"About the war."

"Oh, I see." ('The war and his experience in it,' she thought. 'Unreadable.')

And now (the landscape opening always like a

succession of fans) cows moved deep in buttercups, hedges were dense and creamy with elderflower and cow-parsley. Yet her pleasure in it all was ruined, first by the incident at the junction, and now by the interruption of this man, sitting opposite her, his arms folded across his chest, his eyes never leaving her.

"What experiences did you have?" she felt obliged to ask. "What were you? What did you do?"

"Dropped by moonlight half-way across France. Sat between Gestapo men in trains, with my transmitter in a case on the rack above, hid in cellars while they searched for me overhead . . ." he broke off, looking excited, as if he were listening to this story, not telling it. . . . "Oh, the sound of those footsteps going up and down, wandering away, but always coming back, and sometimes scarcely to be heard above the noises *here* . . ." he tapped his fingers on the side of his head . . . "the rushing sounds that come from too much straining to hear. And it all being so much like the books I read as a boy—passwords, disguises, swallowing bits of paper, hiding others in currant buns . . ."

'So *that* is the sort of man who did it!' she thought, staring back at him.

"You must have great nerve," she suggested, trying in this to find an excuse, a reason, for the emptiness in his eyes.

"Not now," he replied. "The end of the war came at the right time for me. The last time I was briefed, a feeling of staleness came over me, a sort of tired horror . . ."

7

"Tired horror!" she repeated, surprised. When he used those words, she could understand it all.

"And won't it all come back, if you write about it? The horror, and the reluctance."

"When it is done . . ." he began.

"To exorcise it, you mean? To drive it out of you, as Emily Brontë drove out Heathcliff, with her pen?"

Either he found this fanciful or distasteful to him, for he glanced out of the window as if dissociating himself from her comparisons.

She at once felt she had sacrificed Emily Brontë, throwing her in as a spur to conversation, uselessly, for the conversation fell into an awkward jog-trot and then stopped.

The skyline flew higher and higher, went up waveringly towards dark clumps of trees, a parapet of earth encircling them like a crown. This landmark, which meant the end of her journey and the beginning of her holiday, always strongly affected Camilla. She took her ticket from her handbag and sat on the edge of her seat.

"The Clumps!" she pointed out, trying to draw his attention away from his newspaper. "We are nearly there."

He looked vaguely out of the window and at last, when the rounded hill had almost gone, said: "Oh, yes, I remember."

And now that her curiosity was at last aroused, he withdrew his attention, turned again to his newspaper and appeared to be reading with complete absorption the account of a murder. Camilla could see the photograph of a dark girl, smiling, amidst the descriptions (she supposed) of violent despatch, dismemberment and ludicrous parcelling-out in luggage-office, lift-shaft or canal.

"They seem incongruous always," she began, leaning a little towards him and indicating the newspaper, "those smiling photographs which they print alongside the horrors."

He glanced at the paper in a puzzled way. "Well, people *do* smile when their photographs are taken . . ."

"I know. But I think we should all have one serious one done, in case."

He smiled politely and returned to his reading.

That such a man should rebuke her for insensibility stung her uncomfortably. She did rather like to be the one to have the fine feelings, and was glad at last to be at the end of the journey, to see a platform running up to meet them and to be able to stand up and smooth her skirt and gather up her belongings.

"I hope you will enjoy your sentimental journey," she said in a patronising voice, as the train ran into shadow and stopped.

"But I shall be sure to see you at the Red Lion," he said, cramming the newspaper into his pocket, glancing round hastily.

"I have warned you already that there *is* no Red Lion. And even if there were," she added, stepping out on to the cool platform, "women never do stay at those places on holiday."

9

He looked up and down the station, uncertainly, she thought: but there seemed plenty to account for that—his loss of nerve which he had described, or simply the fact of returning after a long interval to a once familiar place. There are usually changes; and if there are not it is even stranger.

"Where *do* women stay?" he asked.

"They go to friends as guests. That doesn't cost as much."

Then, as a young woman appeared, carried off her feet almost by a large dog tugging at its lead, Camilla lost interest in her travelling-companion, smiled quickly over her shoulder, and went towards the ticket-barrier.

.   .   .   .

"This *beast*!" cried Liz, struggling and tugging. "Oh, my God, I'll kick its teeth in in a minute. How are you, Camilla my dear? You will have to carry all of that yourself, you know. I have enough to do."

"What *is* it?"

"I don't know. What should you think? Perhaps a mastiff."

They looked down at its rippling, brindled back, its straddling legs.

"Is it yours?"

"My God no! Whatever should I want with a thing like this? *She* made me bring it. Frances. 'He wants a walk,' she said. And now the palms of my hands are lacerated. Look, they are raw." They were indeed a little reddened. "Yes, 'Hotchkiss can go with you to meet the train,' she said at lunch. As if he were a chauffeur."

"Do you think he would bite?"

"I certainly do."

They hesitated at the station entrance. Before them lay the square, glittering in the heat. On the shadowed side of it, a man carrying a case disappeared into the Griffin, whose shuttered façade seemed to suggest faded chambermaids sitting lost at the end of dark corridors, commercial-travellers sleeping off their midday drink on brass bedsteads, utter silence along all the passages, on all the little flights of stairs.

"I can't carry my bag all that way," said Camilla.

"Neither can we go on a bus with *this*." The great dog lay down on the blistering pavement, slobbering and panting.

"I could leave it in the luggage-office, and we can come down after tea, when it's cooler, on the bus."

"She will only say 'Take Hotchkiss with you'. I know she will say that."

"You mustn't be so put upon."

"Guests are for that. They have to do all the wretched jobs not even a paid servant will do—queue for tomatoes, look at photograph albums, read the books in their bedrooms, admire the cabbage-plants. You can't exert that sort of tyranny over anybody but a guest. And all done so sweetly. 'While you're in the town, just pop in for some tomatoes.' I stood for three-quarters of an hour in a queue, sweltering hot, and women sweating and pushing their baskets against the back of my knees. And *talking* to me . . ." Her voice rose indignantly, but Camilla had gone to the luggage-office and returned without her bag.

"And then," Liz continued, as they crossed the square, " 'If you are going for a stroll, take Hotchkiss with you. He's so bored.' "

"What is she doing? Frances?"

"Playing the piano. Her painting is all going wrong. She is in troubled waters. So she plays the piano very loudly. Awful noises come out of it. A great confusion of sound. Dohnanyi. She has her vengeance on the piano. She gives it hell. She really is an absolute bitch to it. But I cannot take its part. Perhaps you will."

"I'll have that Hotchkiss, if you hand him over."

"I was wondering when you were going to offer."

"She *is* our hostess," Camilla pointed out, stopping to wind the leather strap round her hand.

"But see how we pay for it. Summer after summer."

"I love her," Camilla said, starting off again with the dog.

"And I. I love her, too. But she seems to me insufferable, none the less."

"Let us not talk about her any more. Tell me about the baby."

"What is there to say? He is just like a little baby."

Camilla felt that this foolish remark was Liz deliberately trying to belittle her son, as sometimes a nice child will belittle a possession before another child who has nothing.

"It will seem funny him being there," she said.

"Last year scarcely imagined, this year . . ."

"He never cries," Liz put in quickly. "I promised Frances that he wouldn't. And he hasn't."

"He has two days behind him, and a whole month ahead. We shall judge him at the end of that."

"He sleeps . . ."

"Not with us, I hope," Camilla said quickly.

"In that little room at the end of the passage where she keeps her old pictures. He will probably get painter's colic. Oh, the thought of this long peaceful month ahead!" She half-stopped in the middle of the pavement to consider it. "Marriage is such a sordid, morbid relationship!"

"Yours is, because you always will be attracted to the sort of man who is no good to you. The same man over and over again. Good-looking in an obvious sort of way . . ." She suddenly remembered the man on the train and was silent.

"Ah well, for a whole month let's not talk about him. I *did* think, though," she continued, at once disregarding her own instructions, "that a clergyman would have something more in him than was obvious at first glance. But I discovered that there was even less."

"What did you expect?"

"An inner mystery." She laughed. "And then, somehow, it was all made more exciting by his religion. A suggestion of forbidden fruits. When he touched me, it meant much *more* than other men touching me. And they were such very little touches, too. It was all cruel and exciting. When he came into the room, I

13

shook from head to foot. And then, I thought he would be interested in my soul and discuss it endlessly and that would have been a pleasure to me. But he is never interested in what he has. Only in what he may be going to get next week. So all the shaking and excitement stopped. Nothing took its place. And I am left with a rather cold and greedy man sitting at his desk writing notes to other women—casual-seeming little notes which take him hours and hours to scribble off—he balances the paper-knife on his fingers while he weighs the words in his mind. And I sit darning his socks and watching him."

"You go about asking for trouble. I have always said so."

They passed under a railway-arch and that seemed to be the end of the little town. On one side a street, on the other a hot gravelly lane, bordered with dusty willow trees.

"You seem in a very tart and condemning mood," Liz said, walking with bowed head, her arms folded across her chest.

"I'm sorry. Could you now take this Hotchkiss?"

Camilla examined her hands and wiped them against her skirt. "An awful thing happened where I was waiting to change trains, some poor little man threw himself in front of the express, or rather bungled it and fell on the lines at the side; died when they picked him up. I wonder why?" she suddenly asked herself aloud. "Anyhow, made *me* shake more than I would for any clergyman. Upsetting!"

14

"Something more than upsetting, I should say," Liz observed. But then there was a complicated business of climbing a stile and getting Hotchkiss underneath. When they talked again, it was about other things.

CHAPTER TWO

THE COTTAGE was of flint, the date 1897 done in bottle-ends between the bedroom windows. On Sunday evenings the villagers walked past on the other side of the privet hedge and their voices came clearly into the parlour, or else Frances played her piano so loudly that they looked over the gate in wonder. Along the window-sills were cactus-plants in earthenware pots, bluish green, striped ones; some rosetted or jointed; others all cobwebbed over with faint greyish strands. These plants, together or singly, came into most of her paintings, like a signature.

As Camilla put her hand on the gate, she saw a line of napkins above the fruit bushes and, for a reason she had no time to explore, she felt an impulse of fear, which amounted to a cold unwillingness to see her friend's baby, to have to exclaim over it and admire. She would never, she decided, accustom herself to the strangeness of Liz married and a mother. It appeared also that Liz could not accustom her to it, but would try to do so, with absurd tact and understanding, so that already gulfs began to yawn between them.

From under the canopy of a pram a little braceleted arm dipped in the sun. Liz unleashed the dog and ran forward. Camilla followed, slowly, but not as slowly as she wished. She had no experience of babies and no knowledge of what to say. Making an effort, she put out her fingers for the baby to fasten upon. He rolled over, arching his back, and tried to draw her hand to his mouth. His face reddened and the fat-creases in his tanned legs showed white as he stretched.

"What does Frances think of him?"

"It is only a question of whether he cries or not. We have to keep him quiet at all costs."

"We?"

"Or I go home."

Camilla moved away from the pram, bored. "He is a nice little baby," she said.

'Oh, these damned women!' Liz thought going across the lawn towards the house. But the baby now made desperate hooking movements with his arms, turning his wrists in an agony of rage and impotence, and, his face suddenly crumpling and darkening, began to cry. Liz picked him up and stood rocking to and fro with him under a tree. His sobs were a long time dying down and did so in an exhausted way as if he had been crying for hours. 'He will get spoilt,' Liz thought. 'I shouldn't have come.'

Camilla went through the kitchen. On the cool flags the dog was sleeping, lying on his side. And in the stuffy parlour, Frances was sleeping, too. She sat very upright in a chair, her hands clasped loosely in her lap, and she looked, Camilla thought, not just one year older, but as if age had been for a long time gathering

17

itself for a spring and had now quite overcome her. Her face in sleep seemed drawn down from the cheekbones in lines she would not have permitted if she had been awake. Camilla drew back into the dark passage and as she did so Frances stirred.

"Elizabeth!"

"It isn't Liz." Camilla came back into the room. "I never know what to do when people are asleep."

"What you did. Go away and try to forget what you have seen."

The room was unchanged since last year. Two vases of grasses on either side of the clock, a photograph of Liz as a child sitting sedately on a swing and Frances, then her governess, holding the ropes on either side and surrounded by leaves. The edges of the picture blurred and faded away, as if it were a spirit photograph, as indeed Frances's haunted look perfectly suggested.

Now she put her hands with their heavy, mannish rings over her face and yawned.

"So here you are!" she said. "What are you going to do with yourselves? Giggle and gossip, mess up my best bedroom with your bits and pieces, your untidy ways? Read your everlasting novels? Call great people by their Christian names?"

"Go for walks . . ." Camilla suggested.

"You won't get far from a baby who has to be fed every four hours, even if I am willing to stay behind with him. Which I assuredly am not."

"Where do *you* want to go then?" Camilla asked, sitting down beside all the cactus-plants.

"I don't want to go anywhere, but I want to be left in peace."

"Why should you be? No one else is."

"Because I wasted so many years teaching instead of painting. Teaching little girls like Liz, who do nothing better with their learning than read novels."

"Perhaps you taught her badly," Camilla suggested, leaning back in her chair.

"I wasted my time."

"You had the money for it. And you had to live somehow."

"I wasted my time."

"I want to say two things before Liz comes in. Firstly, don't bully her about the baby. If it cries, it cries and you put up with it. She must have a holiday from that man."

"She has married him."

"The other thing is this dog of yours. We don't want to take it for walks."

"You want to be guests and do nothing?" Frances suggested.

"We would rather pay six-and-a-half guineas a week than take him when we go walking," Camilla said untruthfully.

From the kitchen came the sounds of Liz making tea. When Camilla went out to her, she found her working in an impeded way, with the baby over one shoulder.

They drank the tea under a large mulberry tree where the grass was worn, and they plaited their past year together from the tight knot of last summer's holiday. Into this plait they wove Liz's failure at being married, the birth of her son (Camilla looked down at her lap), little tiffs with parishioners, not amounting to much, but threatening greater things of the same kind for the future; then Camilla (and the man in the train had guessed wrongly, for she did not teach but was the secretary at a girls' school) threaded in her strand, bright with amusement—little gaffes at Speech Day (the Bishop's wife trying to drink tea through her veil) or Staff Meetings; the Old Girls' Reunion and how changed they returned to it, for the first were last and the last were first and Lady Lisbourne, who at school had been nothing, condescended to the erstwhile Captain of Hockey, a rough-voiced woman in tweeds. Liz's laughter rang out across the still garden and was echoed by her son who lay on the grass at her side.

And Frances? But she had nothing to contribute, she declared. Only four pictures. All of them the same and none any good. The year had gone in a way which seemed unbearable to the other two, but was not to her. Week succeeded week, no one called; if they wrote she rarely replied; she talked to no one; Christmas was unremarkable except for one or two cards from old pupils, a cake from Liz which she was a month eating and a book from Camilla which she had not found time to read.

"And then tell Frances about your horrid experience this afternoon," said Liz, as if this would finally round off the year and bring them up to date.

"*My* horrid experience?"

"Well, the fact of it being worse for somebody else doesn't stop it from being horrid for you."

"No, I suppose not."

"What was it?" Frances asked.

"A suicide."

She described it briefly, plucking up grass and scattering it as she did so.

"Well?" said Frances at the end.

"That is all. I can never think of incidents as isolated. They always seem to be omens."

"What nonsense," Frances said, staring. "You try to enlarge yourself by everything that happens, even other people's misfortunes. As if you had *special* feelings."

"You hit the nail on the head," Camilla agreed.

"Oh, *there*!" cried Liz, exasperated. "If you are to quarrel all the holiday, I shall . . ." She turned to her baby clasping his ankles in her hand.

They watched her. She was slim and brown and in her crumpled cotton frock looked like a young girl playing with a doll.

"What? *What* will you do?" Camilla enquired.

But Liz was absorbed now and had forgotten. "I shall go and feed Harry," she said and stooped to lift him.

"And I shall go back to my picture," Frances said and wandered down the garden, snipping up a dead flower here and there as she went. At the end of the path was a wooden building which she called her shed, disliking the special names artists give to things, feeling these words contaminated by Bohemianism, by those who talk too much and strike attitudes.

When she had disappeared, Camilla leant back in her deck-chair, her hands clasped behind her head, her eyes closed. She felt forlorn and far away from Liz, but would not follow her, despite the inkling she had that the time to go was now, to sit with her while she nursed her child, to fetch and carry things for it a little, to take it in her arms, that this had to be done now, at once, or it could never be done. But shyness, obstinacy, a great dislike and a great jealousy prevented her. So she lay back and closed her eyes and wondered what attitude she would now strike to protect herself, to enlarge herself, as Frances, who did not need enlarging, had said. 'And I,' she thought at last, bitterly, 'the physical life, the artistic life, all creativeness closed to me, am left to do the washing-up.'

Later in the evening, Liz and Camilla set out again to the town. They sat on the top of a bus and the evening sun poured over them through the dusty windows and great fans of chestnut leaves brushed the glass as they drove close to the hedges along the narrow roads.

"Frances is changed," Camilla said. "Now she seems an old woman and rather frail. A strange thing happened. When I went in first of all, she was asleep. She looked as if she were dead and had been arranged in the chair. Yet when she opened her eyes, I felt for the first time since I've known her, that once she was a child. Before, I could never imagine that. I think her eyes gave me this feeling."

"A very pale clear blue," Liz said.

"And her hair must have been corn-coloured, that rather harsh, frizzy hair."

"Yes, it was."

"I can imagine her sitting in a schoolroom, with her thin hand over her forehead, learning her Greek, or up in the branches of a tree, peering down. I think she had a brother whom she loved. An elder brother."

"Oh, no, she was an only child," Liz disagreed. "How this bus swings from side to side."

"Yes, perhaps after all, I see her more clearly as an only child. The sort of one who *goes* to places to weep, never bursting into tears on the spot, but buried in the long grass, in the apple-loft, the tears soaking through her sleeve, but always in silence and then tidying up afterwards, utterly vulnerable but careful, the world cruelly foreign, and every sound a pain."

"But why should she have been so very miserable?"

"She was never happy until this last part of her life."

"Then perhaps there will be that for us ·also," Liz suggested. "It doesn't sound very promising."

"*You'll* have your children."

"Children?" Liz pretended to flinch at this plural, but her expression was not dismayed. She fell into a comfortable little silence.

"God knows what *I* shall have," Camilla said over her shoulder as they stepped out of the bus.

"Children, too, I daresay," Liz said carelessly.

"Your marriage is not an encouraging example to me. Besides, I have left it too late."

"You are like Dorothea Casaubon in *Middlemarch*."

"Let's go for a drink."

"I am not supposed to drink while I am feeding Harry," Liz said primly.

"And last year you mayn't drink because you were *expecting* Harry. How absurd! Is the whisky supposed to go direct to him, neat, and make him drunk?"

"I read in a book that it is a good thing not to do."

"We have half-an-hour to wait. What do you suggest?"

"If you very much want a drink, I'll have just one beer."

"I *do* very much want one," Camilla said, and led the way at once into the musty darkness of the Griffin, tidying her hair with her hands as she went.

The man from the train was there, as she had supposed he would be. He was leaning over the bar questioning the barman about the town, the district. It seemed to Camilla puzzling that his sentimental journey should have ended in a place to which he was so much a stranger.

She stood there, shaking coins softly in her hand, waiting to be served, and when the barman turned towards her, the other did so also. In the instant before he smiled, she noticed the slightest flicker of alarm on his face. The smile at once covered it up, but it had been there; she could not deceive herself. As if to do more than cover up his first reaction, as if to trample it down and crush it, he came forward and spoke to her.

Liz sat on a high stool, trying not to look curious, and the sight of her doing this delighted Camilla, who watched her through a great gilt-edged mirror.

"Are you comfortably installed?" she asked in a rather challenging, familiar way, which was for Liz's benefit, and which she at once regretted.

"Upstairs, it is like a fairy-story. Nothing has been touched for twenty years." He lowered his voice. "Not clean. All the pictures look as if they have been dipped into soup. It hasn't a clean smell. The bath has a great green stain under the taps. The chest-of-drawers is full of shrunk moth-balls and rusty safety-pins." He spoke in a quiet but over-dramatic voice and Liz, who could not quite hear, looked away towards the open doorway and yawned.

"Then I am glad to be a woman and not obliged to stay here," Camilla said.

"It is all such a maze of stairways and passages, I feel it will be too difficult to go to bed, to find my own room again. I can't tell you . . ."

"This is a friend of mine," Camilla interrupted, feeling something was now due to Liz. "Mrs Nicholson . . ." She paused.

Liz gave a formal little bow and folded her hands in her lap.

"Now that we have one name, we must have some more," he said. "Mine is Richard Elton."

"We met in the train," Camilla said to Liz, as if this explained more than it did. "My name is Camilla Hill."

"A very nice name."

Liz sipped her beer, making it last, like a child with an ice-cream. Seeing her through the great mirror, head bent over her drink, hair swinging smoothly forward, her brown legs twisted round the stool, Camilla felt as if the day had been a dream, that she would come out of it soon, lifting fold after fold of muffling web; for this could not be real—meeting Liz again after eleven months and finding herself so alienated from her that she could show off to her about a man. 'And *this* sort of man!' she thought, glancing at him through the mirror. Their eyes met. Alone in the looking-glass they seemed. They watched, with a steady fascination, as if those two other selves would commit some action independently of them; would among the reflected bottles, the ferns, glasses, turn to one another in the closest intimacy, make some violent impact upon one another which could not be made in actuality.

Camilla lowered her eyes, stood very still, as if now the mirror were going to crack in two. The room tipped and lurched, people's faces ran together, their voices slipping and painful in her ears. One brush of his sleeve against her arm and the bar, she felt, would burst into flame.

Liz was refusing a drink from him, her hand a lid over her glass, as if he might not take her at her

26

word. When Camilla accepted, she fidgeted on her stool, glancing at the clock.

"We have ten minutes," Camilla pointed out.

"But we must get your case."

"Oh, yes, I had forgotten what we came for."

She drank quickly, conscious of their eyes upon her. She felt very nervous and excited without knowing why.

"Good-bye, then." Her glance flashed round the bar, no more taking him in than all the rest.

"I expect we shall meet again," he suggested.

Liz jumped down from the stool and smoothed her frock, which was beyond smoothing.

"Well, that was all rather unlikely," she remarked, as they came out into the empty square. The sun now struck only the façades of the buildings, the leaves at the very tops of trees; windows high up, even brick-work glinted with gold. The clouds were like eggs. The bar now seemed to them to have been cold and dark and ferny, and they felt the soft air on their arms and brows with relief.

"A very unlikely sort of man," Liz continued. "You grumble at *me*."

"I met him on the train," Camilla repeated.

"Yes. You said that before. Why didn't you tell me you were meeting him?"

"But I wasn't meeting him."

"It was scarcely the merest chance. You knew he would be there."

"We had to drink somewhere."

"It is usually the Bear."

"Well no harm has been done," Camilla said, and gave a little laugh. "He seemed to me a most romantic figure," she added, trying to appear naïve, girlish. "Incredible adventures he had through the war—codes, and pass-words and false moustaches."

"I thought he looked like an American film-star," Liz said. "A sort of tough stupidity."

"He is writing a book."

"Well, so are most people. It would be an abnormality if he were not."

"I am not."

"You will when you become better adjusted."

"To what? One has to be adjusted *to* something."

She saw the two faces again, set in the mirror as if they were in a frame, the two pairs of eyes, steady, *met*, just for that second. The bus came and they climbed up the steps and sat down in the front and while Liz talked, Camilla looked out of the window at the roof-tops, the old tiles golden and uneven under the late sun.

"It is so peaceful," Liz said suddenly. "I know he is thinking—Arthur, I mean—of other women, not me. Oh, in the nicest way, you can't imagine. But because I don't have to watch him doing it, I feel at peace. I am lulled by my ignorance."

"He will poison your life."

"He is about the house so much," Liz said restlessly. "I had never realised how he would always be there. From high up like this I can see into people's bedrooms. But they are gone so quickly."

A little girl stood close to a window, nightgowned,

eyes half-hooded, thumb in her mouth. She stood there very still, almost asleep on her feet, too hot to lie in bed. Men in shirt-sleeves trimmed hedges, their wives leaning from upstairs windows conducting shouted conversations with neighbours in front gardens or up at windows also. The snipped privet lay under the railings. Water came arching out of cans on to the dry flower-beds where calceolarias, lobelias wilted. Old women sat on chairs at doors and men carried their beer outside to the pavement. Little girls with thin arms threw balls against the side of the railway-arch, chanting old rhymes. And then, through the arch, it was the country again, and lovers were walking slowly on the gravelly road; the town, the old people and the children left behind, and the quiet fields and their strangeness to one another lying ahead.

"I hope that Harry hasn't cried," Liz said. "If Frances plays the piano, she will wake him."

"What are these paintings she has done?"

Liz said nothing for a moment, then she brought her fists down on her knees and seemed to be trying to find words. "Frightening! Great black and grey and purple and sulphurous pictures. All nonsense. So *different*. When you think . . . all those flowers she used to paint, those lovely cobwebby blossoms, skeleton leaves, the gauziness of them. And now these awful rocky pictures—and how she comes in and plays the piano as if the pictures had got into her, instead of the other way about. At *her* time of life. And that dog, too. It is all part of the general ferocity—the sun wheeling

29

round, violent cliffs and rocks, figures with black lines round them. And all amounting to—just nothing at all."

"The one she painted last summer was the best she ever did. The one of the room with the lace curtains. A very tender light flowing through them."

"Yes, that was what I *call* a picture. Perhaps we always want paintings to be like novels."

"What happened to that picture?"

"A man bought it for a great deal of money, though I don't know how much. You know how she is. She is utterly determined never to behave like an artist, and that refusal to discuss money is part of it."

"Who was the man?"

"I don't know. I only know that he writes to her and that she seldom answers his letters. And once he sent her a piece of lace as a present from somewhere abroad. How suddenly the sun goes."

"I think it goes gradually," Camilla said, looking at the lines of colour across the sky and all the little gold-reflecting clouds.

"The warmth goes," Liz said, chafing her bare arms. "Do you always fall into friendships with men you meet on trains? It seems a new thing in you."

"We were rather thrown together by circumstance, as anything out of the ordinary does tend to throw people together—wars and thunder-storms or a procession or an accident."

"You mean the man killing himself?"

"Yes."

She had talked of it until it had become unreal. Now it was vividly itself again, the sunset, the late hour, bringing it back to her in its first light. Although her train had taken her away from it, the thing was not done with for other people, she suddenly thought. Doubtless, someone wept somewhere, and the man's lonely despair was not less painful because it was over.

"How did you and that man come into it?" Liz was asking. "I forget his name."

"Richard Elton," Camilla said distinctly.

"I can't think how you remember. I never remember names when I have only heard them once."

"It struck me, because it seemed so much the sort of name people don't have. The sort a woman writer might choose for a nom-de-plume, perhaps . . . or for the name of her hero."

"Yes, I see what you mean."

"He and I didn't come into it anyway," Camilla said, answering Liz's question. "But it meant that it was natural for us to speak about it afterwards. How strangely things happen. The peaceful, sunny afternoon, and *that* dropping into it without warning; except perhaps that all peaceful, sunny things should be a warning in themselves. When you were a child did you ever hunt for a lost ball among ferns and leaves and parting them quickly to look . . ." she made a gesture of doing this . . . "come suddenly upon a great toad, sitting there, very ugly and watchful. All the time there, though you didn't know it, under the leaves. The shock, the recoil!"

31

"Did this ever actually happen?" Liz asked with interest.

"I imagine it must have. I have the sensation of it, the quick tinkling of fear in my wrists, when I describe it."

"I think toads are beautiful, anyhow," Liz said, and she stood up, steadying herself until the bus stopped.

In the lane, the cool air flowed between the hedges, almost as if it were a visible thing, like smoke, or water.

"There! She is at it!" Liz said as they came near the cottage. "The loud pedal down and simply hammering. She is getting fierce in her old age, and she will wake Harry and frighten him."

She hastened up the path and Camilla followed her slowly, breathing very deeply the hay-scented air and feeling moths brush by her towards the lamplit window.

．　　　．　　　．　　　．

"I see you have made yourself at home," Camilla said, pushing all Liz's spread-out jars and brushes to one side of the dressing-table and laying about some of her own.

The windows opened into the branches of a pear tree, a beautiful thing, they supposed, in the spring when they never saw it; but now darkly-leaved and throwing a green darkness into the bedroom. Birds burst in and out of its boughs and small crowned pears dropped into the grass below.

Camilla, having asserted herself over the dressing-table, now turned her attention to the darkening garden. Behind her, back in the shadows of the room, Liz sat on a low chair and fed the baby, who, full and contented, turned from her breast and flung out an arm, his eyes wandering, milky dribble running from a corner of his mouth.

When Camilla faced the room again, as she must sooner or later, she thought (since the strangeness with Liz was binding her into intolerable confines), Liz put the baby up against her shoulder and smoothed his back, her other shoulder, her veined bosom half-bare in her opened frock, her hair hanging loose against her cheek. The baby's head bobbed weakly, he belched twice softly and once more the milk ran from his mouth, down Liz's back.

"Surely he has had too much," Camilla suggested, and she came across the room and dabbed at Liz's blouse with a handkerchief.

"Take him!" said Liz, jerking her shoulder back into her clothes, casting round for pins and napkins.

Camilla had taken the baby and held him awkwardly against her. This awkwardness, this hesitation, he at once sensed, and began to stiffen himself and to arch his back. In his struggles, he pressed his wet and opened mouth to her face, and she recoiled a little.

"He is the first baby I have ever held," she said, "I do it badly."

Liz reached forward and took him. When he was pinned into his napkins she carried him away to his cot.

Camilla was in bed when Liz came back, lying with

33

her arms crossed under her head, looking reflective.

"You will have to leave that man," she said so suddenly that Liz was arrested with her petticoat half over her head. When she was clear, she said in a flustered way: "He isn't bad enough for that. He doesn't do anything wrong, you know."

"He will turn you into someone like himself."

"It must always give a woman a queer feeling when her husband is called 'that man'."

"He is that to me," Camilla said simply. "I cannot call clergymen by their Christian names."

"It should seem an easy thing to do."

"I wonder why he became one?" Camilla yawned.

"The beauty of his voice," Liz said coldly, pottering about at the dressing-table.

"I have been feeling we were poles apart."

"I know. It was nothing I could avoid."

"I was jealous of the baby." She exposed the truth, feeling so much depended on making this effort, but at once clouded her words with a laugh. The idea was not illuminated for long enough to show itself to Liz, who got into bed, still thinking of her husband.

"He will write to me, I suppose," she said as she tucked herself in. "But *long* letters, that take no time to write, about engagements and arrangements, and where he ate his meals, dull letters, none of the famous notes, so gay and so teasing, so hastily scribbled off in about three hours of steady concentration and the help of the *Oxford Dictionary of Quotations*. No, none of those ever again to me. But how can he help himself? He has to be like that, always passing on to someone new, and no harm done, he believes. Nothing done. And nothing ever lasting. No one in his life goes back very far, nor has any likelihood of going any distance into the future. But we won't talk about him any more. What I mean is, he hasn't anyone to say 'do you remember' to. I never have heard him say those words. Not as we do. And when he thinks of the future, he thinks of *next week* always. Not tomorrow, nor next year, never of when he will be old, or of Harry growing up; but just next week, when things should at last be coming round the way he wants them. He also loves titled women," she said suddenly and turned off the light.

She had propped the door open with two books, so that she could hear the baby if he should cry. Everywhere about the room, books supported or balanced the furniture, compensated for the uneven floor, wedging mirrors, steadying the dressing-table. Sometimes, Liz and Camilla eased them out of their places and read them—old memoirs, guide-books, poor, faded novels. Through the open door they heard Frances come up to bed.

"In the old days, she used to knock on the wall, to make us stop talking," Liz said.

"Why did we talk so long? What was it all about?"

"We used to give those tea-parties for English literary ladies."

"Yes, of course. And very disintegrating they were! Everything went wrong."

"We planned them so far ahead, in so much detail, and then talked of them for so long afterwards."

"I think it was Charlotte who wrecked them, with her inverted snobbery. The time she told Ivy how much she gave for her lace shawl in Bradford."

"And said it was her best."

"Anne looked down into her lap. I saw her hands tremble."

"Virginia saw, too."

"Charlotte came too early, anyhow. Before we had time to put a match to the parlour fire."

"Emily wouldn't come in at all. She stood up the road and eyed the gate."

"Jane and Ivy came on time. They arrived at the door together and waited there, looking at one anothers' shoes."

"And Virginia was late, and little Katie never came at all."

"She got lost. Who fetched her in the end? Emily, I mean."

"I think we sent George Eliot out for her."

"But she wouldn't co-operate. She wouldn't sit down. She ruined the party with her standing up."

"I felt Virginia was thinking: 'They only give me such cakes as these because they are women, and I am a woman.' "

"And Elizabeth Barrett taking up all the room on the sofa!"

"Her hand going up all the time to her curls reminded me of Captain Hook. I was always surprised to see it *was* a hand."

"Virginia was right to feel wounded about the food. Women are not good enough to themselves. And the indifferent food is the beginning of all the other indifferent things they take for granted," Liz said. And the literary party was dissolved and forgotten and she was back again with her husband.

"That man in the Griffin," Camilla said presently. "I thought he described the place amusingly."

"I thought he seemed to be acting. He was as if he had learnt the words by heart first. They seemed not to belong to him, nor to match the look in his eyes."

"This flair you have for recognising the spurious, it is a pity you never put it to use in your own case."

Liz said wistfully: "I thought for a few seconds that it was going to be like other years."

"It won't be again."

"My opinions about that wretched man—why should they annoy you? How could you care? And if you did, why, you say far worse than that about my *husband*."

"I say no worse than you say yourself."

"I think you do. But you blame me, then, for disloyalty?"

Camilla said nothing. She lay very still in bed.

"I *am* loyal to him, except to you."

"And to Frances."

"To you and Frances, then."

"So loyalty is a question of numbers? Two is all right."

"I have to be up at six," Liz said. "For Harry. So I shall go to sleep, I think."

"Goodnight, then."

"Goodnight."

They both appeared to fall into a deep and steady sleep at once; and then suddenly Liz laughed and said in a changed, a warmer voice: "Goodnight, Cam."

"Goodnight, Liz dear." And as Camilla laughed too, Frances, in the next room, rapped angrily upon the wall.

CHAPTER THREE

"HERE is a beautiful book!" said Camilla, following Liz across the landing.

"Where did you find it?"

"It was wedging the mirror."

She began to read from it, standing in her nightgown in the early sunshine. Liz put the baby back in his cot and began to go downstairs to make tea.

"It is called *Exemplary Women*," Camilla continued, and followed Liz downstairs.

Hotchkiss lay under the table and the kitchen smelt of him. He opened a bloodshot eye sulkily and kept it open, seemed to follow Liz round the kitchen with it.

When Camilla opened the door to let him out, birds burst up out of bushes, flurrying the leaves, plunged into the dense creeper over the walls. The garden was still, soaked with dew, veiled with a pearly light as if sponged with milk. A little tree of morello cherries seemed painted upon the sky, its fruit luminously red like cherries on a hat.

"After the town . . .!" Camilla began, breathing in the sweetness of the garden, "after the soiledness of everything, all you touched greased over, contaminated by other people's hands!" She glanced at the dusty book she was holding and her interest was at once diverted from the beauties of nature.

"Listen, Liz! Here is one for you. 'The Solemnity of Wedlock'. 'For seldom, we fear, does the bride, half-smiling, half-weeping beneath her crown of orange-blossoms, appreciate the character of the sacrifice she has made. Too often does she wake up with a sudden surprise to the awful breadth and depth of the chasm that lies between her wifehood and her maidenhood, the *now* and the *then*. She misses the mother, the sister, the tender felicities of home, the cherished places, the favourite pursuits, the old singleness of heart, the old serenity of mind, the delightful yet sober freedom of her blissful girlish days. She looks around, and unless she loves—loves long and deeply and worthily—she sees a blank and dreary void, and her heart aches with a dumb, dull pain. . . .'"

"You are making it up," said Liz, coming to the door and looking over Camilla's shoulder. "It sounds like Sappho. Quick! The milkman is coming!"

Camilla, in her nightgown, stepped behind the opened door and continued to read. Liz made the tea.

"And here is something for me. 'Surely a cheerful and happy old maid is less to be pitied than a loveless or neglected wife.' And, now, Jeremy Taylor on celibacy."

The milk was left on the doorstep, the footsteps retreated, and Camilla came back into the sunshine.

"Where did Frances get these books?"

"They were her mother's."

They sat on the table and sipped their tea. As the

40

kitchen grew warmer, flies began to circulate or went up and down the windows with a drowsy sound.

.   .   .   .

Frances awoke to her moss-roses. Each morning they annoyed her more, so endlessly repeated on a thick black trellis over the wall-paper, peeling away near the ceiling in places, leaving a powdery-looking but still flowered pattern exposed beneath. Violets, the one before last, Frances decided. Unless periwinkles. She thought about wall-papers, closing her eyes. She had painted many in her time, the great blown roses in the bedrooms of small French hotels: they had come into her pictures of littered chimney-pieces, rooms reflected in mirrors, the crumpled, tumbled beds, the naked girl holding her silk stocking to the light, her skin cream and apricot against the brilliant, the shocking crimsons, pinks, vermilions of the wall. Then sometimes pale satin-striped or faintly wreathed papers in rooms running with gilt and sunlight, so drenched in glitter that even carpets seemed to reflect molten gold. The insides of houses, glimpses out of windows or through windows, the hand she had put out to try to arrest the passing scene. She closed her eyes and bunches of roses were printed for an instant, startlingly white upon the darkness, then faded, as the darkness itself paled, the sun from the window coming brilliantly through her lids. Trying to check life itself, she thought, to make some of the hurrying everyday things immortal, to paint the everyday things with tenderness and intimacy

41

—the dirty café with its pock-marked mirrors as if they had been shot at, its curly hat-stands, its stained marble under the yellow light; wet pavements; an old woman yawning. With tenderness and intimacy. With sentimentality, too, she wondered. For was I not guilty of making ugliness charming? An English sadness like a veil over all I painted, until it became ladylike and nostalgic, governessy, utterly lacking in ferocity, brutality, violence. Whereas in the centre of the earth, in the heart of life, in the core of even everyday things is there not violence, with flames wheeling, turmoil, pain, chaos?

Her paintings this year, she knew, were four utter failures to express her new feelings, her rejection of prettiness, her tearing-down of the veils of sadness, of charm. She had become abstract, incoherent, lost. 'I am too old,' she thought, and then: '"It wasn't *me*," as women say, when they find the hat they are trying on is beyond their purse.'

Just then, Camilla came in, still wearing her nightgown, and carrying a cup of tea in one hand, a letter in the other.

"It is time to wake up," she said.

"Have you no dressing-gown, Camilla?"

"No."

She put her face into a great bowl of pink and red sweetpeas on the bedside table.

"There is a macintosh of mine you can borrow."

"A macintosh? But it isn't raining. And if it were I shouldn't go out in my nightgown."

"I don't like to see you walking about the house like that."

Frances sat bolt upright in bed and re-tied a ribbon at her wrist, using one hand and her teeth.

"I'll go and dress. You look like a little girl in bed, Frances. Liz has a letter, too. From her husband. A very, very long letter and she is still reading it. It started off 'My dearest wife,' she said. Just as if he had several."

"No man stands a chance against you two. All that running to one another and giggling. You make fun of all the things you fear."

"That's very clever of you," Camilla agreed, and hid her face once more in the sweetpeas. "We are not smiling *through* our tears, but at them."

"Cowardice," Frances murmured, slitting open the envelope, which had a French stamp, and drawing out several sheets of thin paper. Camilla, her face still among the flowers, lifted her eyes for a second and then lowered them.

"Well, I must dress myself," she said, straightening her back.

"I wish you would. Don't be slovenly, dear."

"No, Miss Rutherford. You weren't *my* governess, you know. By the way, why did you never marry any of your employers?"

"Their wives wouldn't have liked it," Frances said, smiling at her letter.

"Surely they knew better than to survive childbirth?"

"No, they seemed not to know."

43

"You would think literature would have taught them as much."

"*Literature* would not."

"Before you begin all that about novel-reading, I will dress myself."

"You keep saying you are going to. But, one moment!"

She held up her hand to stay Camilla as she read her letter. At last, she laid it down on the quilt and said: "Do you think there might be an hotel in the town where I could book a room for someone?"

A curious wary, yet excited look flickered over Camilla's face.

"I'll enquire for you," she said.

"The Bear?"

"Or the Griffin."

"The Bear is reckoned to be the better, I believe."

"All right," Camilla said cautiously. "And who is this who must have the best of everything? Not one of your late employers? At last widowed?"

"No. A Mr Beddoes."

"A Mr Beddoes. I see." She did not see, and was nettled by curiosity. "And when? And for how long?"

"On this Sunday. Tell them for a week to begin with."

"A week to *begin* with," Camilla murmured. "It's going to be a hot day. A long, hot day." She stretched her arms up and suddenly dropped them to her sides and went out, leaving Frances to finish her tea and read her letter through again.

In the bedroom, she took off her nightgown and poured cold water out of a painted jug into a cracked bowl. It was soft water, but grit sank through it to the bottom. Standing barefooted on the rush mat, she soaped her arms, leaning over the washhand stand, rinsed in the beautiful, silken rain water and dried herself on a very old fluffy towel.

The morning promised well, she decided, fastening her cotton frock. With a little arranging, the morning promised very well.

She took up a book to wedge the mirror and began to brush her long light-brown hair. She knotted it back as usual and then unknotted it and rolled it all up on the top of her head, at once becoming a different woman and ready to behave differently to match.

.   .   .   .

As soon as Liz had settled down to bathing the baby, Camilla came into the kitchen swinging a basket and looking casual.

Liz unwrapped the steaming napkins from the child's thighs and glanced up suspiciously.

"Where are you off to?"

"Frances gave me a job to do in the town."

"What sort of a job?"

"To book a room at the Bear for a Mr Beddoes."

"Or the Griffin?" Liz suggested. She crooked her arm under the child's back and lowered him into the bath of water. "Surely the Bear will be full?"

"I shall have to find out," Camilla said, lightly,

thinking that now there would have to be another, subtler excuse.

"Or you thought Frances *said* the Griffin," Liz continued, laving the baby's limbs, and her hair trailing over and touching the water. "You muddled the two names." She thought she would punish Camilla for a little while. "What a lot one gives up in motherhood," she sighed. "One mayn't even go and help to book a room for Mr Beddoes. Mr Beddoes! I have heard the name somewhere. I wonder where."

"We shall find out. It cannot be kept from us much longer, for he is to arrive this very Sunday."

Frances came into the room, affecting not to have heard, but Camilla blushed. She looked awkwardly into her basket for a moment and then said she must be off.

Frances stood looking down at the baby lifting his legs and splashing them into the water, his eyes brightening at such power. Just as Camilla got to the door, she said casually, without lifting her head: "Oh, take Hotchkiss with you, my dear. It will do him good."

"But will it do *me* any good? As a matter of fact, he is beyond my control."

"I should like him to go," Frances said quietly, and Liz smiled to herself and lifted her baby out of his bath, holding him high in the air in a movement of triumph; he screamed with excitement and ecstasy, and the water ran down Liz's arms and over the floor.

Camilla wound the dog's chain round and round her hand and set off down the lane behind him. He nosed

46

the ground, as if he were a bloodhound. He broke into a lumbering sort of trot and Camilla came hastening along behind him, jerked at the end of the chain, hot, unsteady, and her hair, she felt, all ready to collapse.

She went along quickly, and not entirely because of Hotchkiss, but also because she felt she was escaping, escaping Liz and Frances, escaping the two she loved, probably, most in her life, and avoiding the long, leisurely morning she had looked forward to in other years, the endless, sunny, gossipy, holiday morning, with the apples to peel, peas to shuck, coffee under the mulberry tree, shopping at the post-office. What had seemed plenty in other years, now appeared thread· bare. She felt a restlessness, like milk beginning to sway up to the boil, a trembling excitement, sometimes pleasurable as it had been in the Griffin last night; but often painful, as it was when she held Liz's baby or watched Liz with him. She knew that what had charmed her in other summers could not charm her now; and felt that, because of this, the holiday must be different and had been different from the beginning, different at the railway station, at her arrival, different with Liz. The long series of these summer holidays from girlhood onwards was suddenly broken. Or had it begun to break last year, with Liz retching her heart up every morning, weeping at night, frightened, alien, yet important? Frances, too, had changed. She had aged more than twelve months. She had painted those pictures. She had added this dog to herself.

Camilla stopped and wound the chain on to the other

wrist. Hotchkiss lay down on his back in some horse-droppings and rolled his great body from side to side, while Camilla tugged and cursed at him. Cursed at Frances. At herself, for not having gone to Switzerland with the Science mistress instead of this.

As she came into the town, the dog gave up running ahead and now lagged, nosing at gateways, standing still to bark at nothing, exploring, loitering, becoming entangled with prams and passers-by. The streets were busy. Women in cotton frocks drove in from the surrounding villages to stand in fish-queues, drink coffee in tea-shops and park their cars in the wrong places.

The pavements were hot through her sandals, traffic flashed and glittered, the humid scent of bread-baking, so beautiful in winter, was sickening in the heat. Flies danced over the block of ice at the fishmonger's, crawled on the great blue and silver heaps of mackerel, the orange kippers. Stale tobacco and last night's beer-spillings was the smell at the Griffin, even in the dark, druggeted hall-way. Here the crimson walls bur-geoned with antlers, with horns, with glass-eyed heads and plump and luminous fish encased among linen weeds. Camilla suddenly shivered. Hotchkiss lifted his leg at an umbrella-stand and she hit him across the back with the chain. He growled and turned his blood-tinged eyes upon her.

No one came. The hotel seemed enfolded as a cocoon, indifferent to life, but still a little active in itself, for a clock ticked with an oily, solid sound at the foot of the stairs; far, far away there was a gentle clatter of washing-up; in the courtyard, empty barrels were trundled across cobblestones.

Presently, a thin elderly man came out of an office, a dry shuck of a man in a neat alpaca jacket, *The Times* folded under his arm.

"Is there anything I can do for you?"

Camilla jerked Hotchkiss away from the umbrella-stand and asked to book a room: moreover, she insisted firmly, she must see the room itself before she did so. It must be quiet, quiet yet airy. Mr Beddoes, she seemed to know beforehand, would be old and faddy.

Hotchkiss followed them upstairs, clawing the drugget. They ascended into a region of hushed darkness, uneven floors, loose boards: taps dripped behind doors, mice rattled along the wainscoting. No visitors emerged from the rows of closed and numbered doors, still less Richard Elton, but for whom Camilla would have been booking a room at the Bear, rather more carelessly.

Frances might have been pleased with the room into which Camilla was eventually shown. It looked like one of her early paintings, with its collapsing brass bedstead, its black, scratched floor-boards and rush mats. Neat grey towels, much darned, hung from a rail; immensely long-handled pokers and tongs and shovels were laid out before the tiny fireplace with its fan of damp and sooty paper and its old cigarette-ends. A wicker-chair uncoiled in long fronds; a vast waste-paper-basket awaited a lifetime's letters. But the room

49

was quiet. It was quiet as the tomb. From the window, she could see whole streets of slate roofs winding away up the hill like stretched accordions, and beyond these were fields with their blueish trees and ovals of shade.

"A splendid view of the clumps," the proprietor pointed out, as if he were the proprietor also of those knots of trees on the horizon, which must reflect credit on his hotel, enhance this bedroom. Indeed, it was sensible of him to direct her attention *out* of the window, and then on above the roof-tops.

"Saxon earthworks," he continued.

"How interesting," Camilla murmured.

Having thus established the desirability of age, the glory of old things, he felt able to draw back from the window and allow her to look at the room again. It was as if he had linked the crumbling, ancient furniture to the Saxon earthworks. He made her feel that in such a district newer things would be out-of-place.

Camilla put her hand dutifully on the bed. The mattress did not give. But she now felt that Mr Beddoes must fight his own battles. He was a stranger to her, and she had only used him as it suited her; although to little purpose, she thought, following the man back along the silent corridors where the sun lay over threadbare carpets. To very little purpose, she reflected, glancing in all directions.

Downstairs in the vestibule, she lingered at the desk, spelling out Mr Beddoes' name very slowly, she supposed correctly: but the hotel was enfolded in quiet and no one came,

"Could I get a sherry?" she asked suddenly, looking desperately round.

The proprietor felt warm towards her—a woman with agreeable ways, who had admired his best view, overlooked his worst bed, and now asked for sherry at eleven o'clock in the morning. Skirting Hotchkiss warily, he opened a door and she found herself once again in the saloon, but on the other side of the bar, where the barman sat reading a newspaper. He sprang up at once, lifted the flap of the counter for her and wiped it down with a damp cloth.

"A sherry for madam," the proprietor ordered.

The bar was empty. She sat on a high stool and sipped her sherry. The street door stood open and the shadows of passers-by crossed the wedge of sunlit linoleum. There was the sound of traffic, the constantly approaching and fading footsteps, the shuffling and the murmuring of people going by.

A newspaper-boy came in and threw a late night extra across the bar. Camilla bought a paper and glanced at the headlines. The barman turned at once to the back page.

'I shall have to go,' she thought, with lingering sips at her sherry. 'It looks peculiar for me to be sitting here.'

She felt shamed and deflated at her behaviour, especially humiliated when she considered the reason for this behaviour, the rather contemptible man who began to obsess her, to engage her thoughts, to be used as a weapon against Liz and who now walked in from the street as if his steps had led him towards her all the morning.

Again, fear was the first change on his face. First, he was not glad to see her, and then, as if he recollected something, very glad. He smiled his film-star smile, waved the bunch of mint he was holding, and at once gaiety broke over them, even over the barman, who had, apparently, been awaiting him. A great drinking session had been planned between them.

"You are just in time. In the very nick of time," Camilla was assured.

The barman lifted the flap again and Richard went round behind and, holding his bunch of mint under the tap, called for ice and for double whiskies. The barman gave a few anxious glances at the door, but soon surrendered to the general gaiety.

"But no, I couldn't!" Camilla cried. "After this sherry, I couldn't."

"Sherry!" he said scornfully. "Discount the sherry. What a fine dog. Oh, what a beauty he is! Hello old boy!" He set the mint-julep in front of Camilla and bent down to Hotchkiss, who slavered gratefully.

Camilla smiled. "He *is* rather," she heard herself saying. And to hide her own amusement at herself, took up her new drink so suddenly that ice rattled against her teeth.

"Nice?" he asked, glancing up at her.

"Very—refreshing," she gasped.

The sprig of mint was wreathed and encrusted

with bubbles, as if these were crystal leaves embedded in a glass paper-weight.

"I like your hair that way."

At once, of course, her hands went up, began to twist in loose strands.

"It is very untidy."

"I like women's hair to be untidy. Not to feel that the hair is more important than the woman."

She flushed and turned her head and, as she did so, her throat moved.

"Women become different people each time they change their hair style," he went on, seeming determined, as some men are, to enlarge the gulf between them and yet by this very measure to bring them closer together, to make her conscious of her womanhood above all else, and by heightening those differences between them, underline what seemed to him the one way of resolving them.

This underlining Camilla had hitherto despised. Now, like the mint-julep, it seemed an experiment that might be made. It could, in fact, add something to her: enhance her importance. A fear of being left out inspired her, a feeling that life was enriching everyone but herself, that education had taken the place of experience and conversation the place of action.

She knew, as she embarked on what she vaguely hoped might be a small adventure, that a girl in her 'teens would have managed more adroitly than she, would have been better supplied with badinage and ready-made phrases. And for a girl in her 'teens, she thought, there would also have been some excuse for growing so preoccupied with a man of this kind –the excuse that he was handsome (she thought 'handsome' was just the word for him) and that he was assured and easy in his manner. Too assured, too easy, for Camilla at her age. But girls in their 'teens admire those who manage so much better than they can themselves. He behaved, she decided, like someone who has spent his childhood in India with those who look only at the top-most layer of life, judge by the appearance of this, are reassured, and thus harden into indifference, become calloused over by preconceptions, until finally, no shaft of truth is sharp enough or barbed enough to strike through their stupidity, their bitter platitudes, their easy divisions of mankind, their way of converting religion rather than being converted by it. All, she thought, circling the whisky about the smoothing ice, all that I most detest.

He now sat down beside her and fondled the dog who slobbered over his hand, looked trustingly up at him.

"Were you brought up in India?" Camilla suddenly asked him.

"In India?" He looked suspicious and surprised. "No. Why?"

"Oh, I often amuse myself fitting people against backgrounds."

"No. My people were in the Philippines, but I was sent over to school when I was ten."

'Yes,' she smiled to herself, 'he would always say "people", not "parents". And how exactly right I

54

was. India or the Philippines, there's no difference. They have the same effect.'

"I daresay you found the natives a useless lot?" she asked dryly.

"Bone-idle, my dear girl, bone-idle."

The boy of ten easily dismissed the Philippinos, and added: "Foully dirty crowd, too. There's nothing to be done with them. Die like flies."

"I suppose it's the cheap labour . . ." Camilla went on, as if she were tickling a trout.

"A fallacy. Don't you believe it. I've seen it and I know. The truth is, I've watched twenty of them laying a piece of concrete a couple of English navvies'd do in less than half the time."

"You think very highly of English labourers?" she suggested, and tipped her glass until there was only ice left in it.

"Perhaps. In comparison," he said cautiously. "And there are plenty of exceptions. Let's have some more drinks, George."

The barman's name, she suspected, was not George, but he answered to it in the cause of *bonhomie*.

A Siamese cat entered the bar from the street. Very delicately it picked its way across the linoleum, one paw before the other, swaying with unborn kittens. Hotchkiss growled and dribbled. The cat leapt clumsily to the bar and sat in a corner, licking the smell of beer from its feet. When this was done, she put all four paws together and, stretching high with arched back, opened her mouth in a yawn like a pink gladiolus.

55

"Elegant even in the family way," Camilla observed.

"That damned thing!" Richard said. "It belongs to old Pussyfoot." The barman was obviously appreciative of this description of his employer. "My God! the noise it makes. Am I right, George, or am I not?"

"True enough, sir."

"The difference between 'sensual' and 'sensuous'," Camilla said, and glanced from Hotchkiss to the cat, but she might have been talking to herself. "What is her name?"

"Petronella," the barman said as if embarrassed. Then suddenly both men doubled up into unaccountable laughter.

"Give me a dog any day," Richard said, sobering for a moment in order to make this patriotic remark—for such Camilla understood it to be.

The cat licked her creamy bib, blandly, contemptuous.

"The sort of animal that horrible old fairy *would* have," Richard said.

The barman thought he had excelled himself. He wiped his eyes on a tea-cloth.

In the middle of their laughter, Camilla felt suddenly that it was all impossible. 'I am not like that,' she thought, 'I don't behave like that, and I must never behave like it.'

Under the cover of some people entering the bar, he turned suddenly to her—and it was as if he had awaited the opportunity—and in a low voice said: "You should learn to forget yourself, you know. How can you enjoy life if you are always to be on your dignity?"

To her astonishment, she felt curious, not insulted. The look he turned on her was one which women very different from herself might have been flattered to receive. She realised that for all his worldliness and his stupidity, which she had just been testing, he knew about her. It is pleasant to be read like a book. We can always accept what is pleasant and explain away— we hope—the reverse: and, at least, it is the beginning of a conversation. That he considered an understanding of women to be a part of his worldly-wisdom she did not know, because she had never been so close to worldly-wisdom before.

"Why do you say I am on my dignity? Is it because I haven't laughed at your jokes?"

He looked troubled.

"But you're right. I am—unbending, afraid of making a fool of myself. Haven't your confidence."

"I don't know about confidence," he said in agreement. "But the life I've led . . . no one ever sheltered me. I fought my own battles always."

She saw him cornered by bigger boys, his fists going quickly up, his eyes above them over-bright. Yet why should the boys have cornered him at all? He was not delicate or deformed or in any way an obvious victim. No, they had cornered him for cheek, for 'cockiness'. They had been about to teach him a lesson. What he had defended himself against, he had first provoked. And he had never learnt his lesson. When he talked to the barman, when he spoke of the Philippines, when he made her feel so conscious of being a woman, it was obvious that he had not learnt his lesson. He would always take advantages. He had neither the pride to scorn them, nor the humility to step aside. He would take his advantage and rub his hands with satisfaction— social advantages, the advantages of the strong fist, the ready tongue; advantages over women. Yet he is stupid, she thought. I tickled him like a trout. It was my secret pleasure. He has never had his lesson because he was always strong, sharp, and worldly-wise. No one pierced his armour, for he was much less vulnerable than anyone else. Only a subtler mind than his could find the right weapon, and the subtler minds would have left him alone.

'Then what do I want with him?' she suddenly asked herself, staring dully into her glass. 'Why should I care? Is it to punish him? But he did no harm to me.' He did plenty of harm to others though, she guessed. 'Plenty of harm. It is all over his face, the harm he has done. Is it not, also, just a little to punish Liz, that I sit here, came here in the first place, avoid her? Because I feel she has shut me out.'

"What about that book of yours?" she asked him.

"Book?"

He put his hand out for her glass, as if to give himself time. He was indeed, she thought, slow-witted for a secret agent.

"No, I don't want any more to drink. I must go home." She put her glass on the table.

"I haven't started it yet. I find it difficult . . . to know how to go about it. I'm a man of action, no literary gent."

His conversation had many of these *passé*, slangy touches; as if he would even rather be old-fashioned than straightforward.

She stood up and began to re-wind Hotchkiss's chain round her hand. The cat sat washing her face, her black paw curving over and over her nose. As the dog moved, she put her four feet quietly together, brought her eyelids close and was perfectly still, like a little stone cat on a gatepost. Yet her waiting seemed to tick inside her.

"I have to go out to get a paper," Richard said, standing up, too. "I'll walk as far as the newsagent's with you."

As he passed the cat on his way out, he suddenly slapped his hand down in front of her on the bar so that she blinked, was unsteadied by a different fear from the one she already had.

"Why did you do that?" Camilla asked in the street.

"Do what?"

"Frighten the cat."

"Like making the damn thing jump."

"You think it is manly, English, of you to hate cats."

"S'right," he said carelessly.

"You used to tease them as a boy."

" 'Tease' is *one* word." He grinned. "I always liked a dog. Had a fox-terrier for years when I was a lad. How many miles we walked together, God knows. Faithful little beast. 'Cats!' I'd say, and he was away like lightning after them."

They passed a newsagent's shop.

"My father once gave me a thrashing and all the time the dog cried outside the door, and when I came out he jumped up and licked my hands. I never forgot that. A child isn't ever really lonely if he has a dog."

"Were you lonely?"

"Yes," he said briefly.

"Your father . . ."

"He was a drunken swine. I wasn't the only one he laid about. My mother got her share, too."

"There's a boy selling papers!"

He held up a coin and the boy came running to him. Still walking along with her, he opened the newspaper and read the front page, peeped a little inside and folded it up carefully and put it in his pocket.

For the first time, she felt his sensibility counted after all.

"Those beatings," she began, "but don't tell me if you don't care to . . . did they harm you very much? Does wielding the rod spoil the child?"

"They cut me off from other children. And then, one's mother running into the garden in her night-gown . . . other parents stop asking you to tea, you get left out of the birthday-parties. There is something not *quite* . . . in any case, they don't ask you. When they meet you in the street, they are over-kind, solicitous, give you sixpence, but they still don't want their children to mix with you . . . the ugliness you might uncover . . . ruining all the sweetness and light. So you are left out for ever. And for ever. You are left with just the dog."

"He let you have the dog . . . your father, I mean," she pointed out, as if there must be something to be said for everybody.

"The dog was a good way of punishing me," he said, easily disposing of her fallacy. "When he beat me, I'd never cry, not when I had weals down the backs of my legs and couldn't sit in my bath. But when he thrashed the dog, I screamed with nerves and blubbered."

'I blamed him,' she thought, 'for not being humble. And all the time it was I . . . 1 was the bumptious, judging one, the sarcastic, clever and superior one.' As we do not apologise for our thoughts, or only when they are solidified into words, she said nothing, but she felt depressed and ashamed.

"What happened to your mother?" she asked, and gave a quick little glance down from the corner of her eyes, not at him, but in his direction. This look—Liz knew it well—was a sign that she was deeply moved, but embarrassed.

"She died . . . she just gave up living. It was as if she suddenly lay down and turned her face to the wall and stopped breathing. Heart failure they put it down to. How right they were!"

"Yes, I see."

They came to the railway-bridge, and the country lay on the other side.

61

"Shall we meet again?" he suggested, slowing his pace. "Will you come for a drink again?"

"I expect I shall."

"When?"

"Perhaps tomorrow evening."

"Will you bring your friend?"

She betrayed nothing, she thought: not a flicker of annoyance or disappointment. "If you like," she said evenly.

"Well . . ." he began. He shrugged. Then: "Don't," he said. "Come alone. Will you come alone?"

"I'll see."

They were standing quite still now, and the shadow of the bridge was cold on her arms. Suddenly, overhead, a train thundered and pounded and was gone. When they could speak again, he said: "Tomorrow evening then. I'll be in the bar."

He turned and walked back the way he had come.

'And now,' thought Camilla, coming out into the sunshine again, 'now for the lies and excuses.'

Her eyes ached in the bright sun. Even Hotchkiss glowered and slouched in the midday heat which bleached the gravelled road and sharpened the bands of shadow which fell across it from the poplar trees.

CHAPTER FOUR

Liz sat under the mulberry tree. The fruit was scarlet and black among the dark leaves. Outside this circle of shade, the garden burned and blazed with the hot colours of the bean-flowers, of montbretia, golden-rod, geraniums.

'My dear Arthur,' she had written on a piece of paper; but it had blown away across the flower-border, and, too lazy to fetch it, she had begun again on another sheet.

'My dearest Arthur' (although, she thought, just as he has only one wife, so I have only one Arthur). 'I am glad you enjoyed your nice evening at Lady Morrison's, and very sorry that I forgot to give you her message before I left. Harry has settled very well and Frances is delighted with him. Camilla has arrived, and we are having a peaceful holiday—just like the old days. I wish you were here,' she was adding, but the wind, like God Himself, wrenched away the paper from her at this lie (indeed the letter was a series of lies) and wafted it into a lavender hedge.

She gave up, lay down among all the squashed mulberries with her arms under her head and fell asleep.

Her husband wakened her. He stood over her,

63

wearing his best grey suit, his neat smile. She felt at
once ungainly, crumpled, put the back of her hand to
her mouth, as if she must have been dribbling, shook
her hair from her forehead. A look of annoyance
gathered in her eyes.

"Arthur, how nice! Why are you here?"

"*You* are why I am here, of course."

"Does Frances know?"

She glanced at the cottage, as if friends fail unless
they can stave off one's husband.

"No one was at home, I thought."

(Frances was excused.)

"You are glad to see me," he said.

"Glad . . . why, yes. A little put out . . . to wake
and . . ."

"But you *are* glad?" he insisted.

She picked a squashed mulberry from her leg. When
she looked up, she saw that he held a piece of paper
behind his back. Her letter, which he had found lying
across his path, he had read. Seeing it addressed to
him, he considered it already his property, forgetting
that we must not be held to account for letters we have
not posted—a thing he, of all men, should have
remembered.

He held it up and read out in his very low and
melodious voice . . . "a peaceful holiday, just like
the old days. I wish you were here." He folded
it and slipped it into his pocket. "You look rather
dishevelled, Elizabeth. Your wish has come true, so
show your pleasure."

"How do you do," said Frances coming up the path from the shed in a hideous flowered apron. "How kind of you to call!" She put out her hand and then glancing apologetically at Liz, said: "This is a friend of mine, who is staying with me . . ."

"Dear Miss Rutherford, she is also my wife."

"Don't you recall that wedding, Frances?" asked Liz, brushing her skirt busily. "Did you never see those unruly curls before, nor hear that boyish chuckle? That wedding . . . the bride had half a glass of champagne (Frances frowned at her pronunciation) "to her head—yet was it the champagne, after all?"

"Champagne," Frances cut in.

"Champagne," Liz said mechanically, a poor imitation.

"I remember now and I apologise. I simply was not expecting you," Frances reproved him.

His life was made up of dealing with old ladies. "You bore the shock better than my wife," he said lightly.

"But where can you *sleep*?" Liz cried. "There is hardly room for Harry and even Mr Beddoes we must put up at the pub."

"And who is Mr Beddoes?" he inquired, with a benevolence with which he hoped to cover his curiosity, a jocularity grown-ups often use when they ask impertinent questions of young children.

"Mr Beddoes is a film director," Frances said. "Where are you off to, Elizabeth?"

65

Liz had scarcely moved her feet, but her body had seemed about to fly away.

"Harry," she said hastily, thinking there are advantages in motherhood. She was wanting to run to Camilla with this astonishing piece of news, and now walked fretfully across the lawn with her husband to Harry's pram. Arthur stood with his hands clasped loosely behind his back, watching the baby, determined to use no baby-language, to be impartial and detached. Nothing resulted. His son rolled away from him stretching and kicking, until his eyes grew calm watching the movement of leaves. It is not possible to act as man-to-man with an infant.

Frances left them and they stood on either side of the pram looking down at their child.

"Liz, darling, I came to ask a favour of you, not to stay. I have to get back some time tonight."

"What is the favour?" she asked, not looking up.

"I want you to come home tomorrow . . . just for tomorrow."

She looked up quickly. "Why?"

"I want you to give the prizes at the social tomorrow night. They asked for you to do that. You can return later. Come back with me now, go to the hairdresser's in the morning and we'll think out a little speech between us . . . a very short one . . . something simple and amusing and informal." (She had better not try to stand on her dignity, he thought.)

"A speech?"

"I will help you."

66

"But I couldn't make a speech. Women don't make speeches."

"Oh, don't start all those generalisations about men and women," he said wearily, thinking her holidays did her no good, reinforced her obstinacy.

"Well, there must be plenty of other women who could give the prizes. Lady Davidson, for instance."

"Well, naturally, they approached Lady Davidson first, but it is her psychology night."

"Psychology night?" Liz repeated.

"She goes to lectures on psychology," he said briefly, and shut his eyes to hide his impatience.

"It is a compliment that they should have asked you. And—more than that . . ." he flushed and put a hand down to the pram and touched his son's head . . . "it would be a way of . . . I am afraid that some of the parishioners feel it odd that you should have left me *just* now . . . with all the trouble about the dry rot in the north wall . . . and after that contretemps about the magazines they think . . . it would help me," he said, becoming more manly. And then, very simply and looking across at her for the first time . . . "It would help to save my pride."

"Why did you marry me, Arthur?"

'She is so warm,' he thought, 'so impulsive, her arms went round me quickly with a child's reckless embrace, as sweet as honey, alive, relaxed like a little cat.' But warmth, impulsiveness, recklessness, sweetness, are advantages in a wife only if they turn inwards upon the home, the husband. And what has always flowed widely, easily, is not so suddenly canalised. Then, too, how often those qualities reflect *too* warm a nature, indicate lack of discrimination, promiscuity in its widest, if not its narrowest sense?

"Because I loved you, my dear. Will always love you."

"But how will it help you for me to go against my nature, make a fool of myself?" He glanced at her creased frock, her untidy hair. "Oh, I know, I know! But I like to be a fool in my own way," she cried. "Everybody does."

"It is an unpardonable word anyhow. A blasphemy against God."

"God must be brought into everything, into every conversation we ever have."

He looked wounded, stubborn.

"Oh, I'll do anything, anything—scrub the Sunday-School floor, hem all those damned garments, clean the brasses, dig graves," she cried, her voice rising shakily, "but not the things I *can't* do."

"Don't be childish," he said sharply, condemning the quality he had first loved in her. "I've asked you to do nothing difficult or unsuitable; only to take your place beside me as a wife. There is no need to cry and wring your hands."

"I haven't changed."

"That's beside the point. We are all changing from one minute to the next."

"But the core of us remains the same."

"And marriage changes us quite. How can we enter

68

marriage and remain the same? The circles of our existences become concentric."

"Tea is ready!" Frances called from the kitchen doorway.

"Tea is ready," Liz repeated to her husband, as if she were the interpreter.

They moved away from the pram towards the house. Harry began to cry, but they scarcely heard him.

In the dark parlour, the best china was spread out. As there was a man to tea, the crusts were cut off the sandwiches. Honey ran out of a broken comb on to a painted plate. In the middle of the table, a cactus was in flame-coloured bloom. The flowers sprang from its finger-tips as if by accident.

Liz went up to call Camilla. She was lying on the bed asleep, a book under her cheek. When she sat up, there was the deep impression of it across her face.

"I do feel like hell. So thirsty."

The light hurt her eyes, and she put her hands up as Liz shifted the curtains.

"Arthur's downstairs."

"Arthur?"

"Yes."

"Good God."

"Cam, darling, you must support me . . ."

Camilla went to the dressing-table and began to comb up her hair.

"What does he want?"

"He wants me to make an exhibition of myself. I am unable . . ."

"Tell me *quickly*!" Camilla said, her mouth full of hairpins.

"He wants me to give away prizes at a social . . ."

Camilla's eyes, now more accustomed to the light, stretched wide with surprise and laughter. She looked at Liz through the mirror, but Liz looked away.

"And make a speech," she added.

"You do it, darling."

"No."

"For fun."

"It wouldn't be fun. We must go downstairs now. You *are* on my side, Cam?"

"I am on your side, if you say black's white and night is day."

"And, Cam, I hope that was a nice room you booked at the Griffin."

"I won't be on your side, if you start all that malicious innuendo again."

"But Mr Beddoes will expect the best."

"And why?"

"He is a film director," Liz whispered, smiling sweetly back from the door of the room.

Camilla followed, still rather dazed from the morning's whisky, rather dulled and maladjusted.

Downstairs, Frances was pouring out, and making conversation. Fifteen years of practice had perfected Arthur at going out to tea. His wife and her friend seemed only to disintegrate the peaceful game.

He had met Camilla before but not with her hair so

elevated. She seemed a new person and brought into the stuffy room a faint smell of whisky, which he found most disagreeable. He thought her influence on his wife harmful, and recognised her ideas prevailing in Liz instead of his own. She sat down too demurely, he thought, as if she were up to some mischief, and he watched her warily, expecting her to begin.

The red mark, which was fading slowly from her cheek-bone, looked as if someone—but surely not Liz—had struck her and gave her, he thought, a faintly exalted look, even feverish.

"Your husband tells me you are going home for a couple of days," Frances said to Liz, as she handed her tea.

"But Liz hasn't said 'yes'," Arthur put in quickly. "It was scarcely discussed."

"Of course she will go," said Frances.

"Do you know *why* I am to go?" Liz asked quietly.

Frances looked up.

"To make a speech," she said. She put some bread-and-butter in her mouth but seemed not to be eating it. Her face was expressionless.

Camilla, who had not spoken before, burst into what she hoped was merry laughter. To Arthur, who was much annoyed, it sounded Satanic.

"And why cannot you make a speech?" Frances asked, as if some doubt had been cast upon her own excellence as a governess. "It is only a wonder that married to a vicar for eighteen months you have not made one before."

"It was Arthur she married, not the vicar," Camilla said, too quickly.

He glanced at her in a measuring way, as if presently he would give his opinion and it would be the right one, and the only one, and well worth listening to.

"Liz will do her duty," Frances said and put a knife into a sad-looking raisin cake as if this must, together with her words, finish the discussion. Arthur, who could eat tea and deal with a situation at the same time, took his slice of cake; Liz, who could not, refused.

"But *duty*!" she cried. "What *is* my duty? And surely I have a duty to myself?"

"Oh, no!" Frances said. "That's loose thinking, my dear. That's a pitfall always. Anything that must be explained won't be your duty. Duty is very simple and obvious. It is nearly always what you don't *want* to do." She glanced at Arthur, as if she thought he could not have put it better himself. He smiled uneasily.

"It will be the thin edge of the wedge," Liz wailed.

"It will be the beginning of the life you chose. All this time, have you done *nothing* to help Arthur?" Frances asked.

"One or two things," Liz said in a low voice, glancing timidly in Arthur's direction. 'The magazines,' she thought, 'the times I was late, the messages I forgot.'

"There has been Harry," Arthur reminded them, "and before he was born poor Liz so very unwell."

('She is unwell now,' he thought. 'Tears too near the surface. And Camilla sees that and she is blaming me, and shows it simply by saying nothing.')

He put his hand out and took his wife's. "Liz darling, if it will go so much against the grain, of course you shan't do it. I will go straight home and only be sorry that I ever worried you."

Camilla frowned. She put a spoon into the honey-comb and honey ran out over the plate.

"I shall go, Arthur," Liz said. "Yes, of course, I shall go. There never was any choice really."

"My dear, there is no choice *now*. It would seem to be forcing you against your will if I let you come, and so you mustn't."

"I shall! I shall!" She knocked over a cup of tea and ran out of the room.

"Such an exquisite fuss about nothing," Frances said, slipping a saucer under the wet table-cloth. "All over a speech!"

"It would comfort us, if we could think it was that," Camilla said.

Her manner was idle, insolent and cool, and her detachment a pretence, he knew. She had been prepared to fight him for a long time, but he had beaten her before she could begin. He saw her almost as an ambassadress of evil, and felt that he had con-founded her, had triumphantly defended against her destructive schemes his position in the world, the welfare of his flock, duty, example, respectability, and the institution of marriage.

Upstairs his wife was crying.

'So worldliness prevails,' Camilla thought. 'So the weak go to the wall!'

In the garden his son was crying, too; but for that not even Camilla could blame him.

CHAPTER FIVE

CAMILLA walked with Hotchkiss along the quiet lanes. Trees and the hedgerows were as dark as blackberries against the starry sky; a little owl took off from a telegraph-post, floating down noiselessly across a field of stubble. Outside the Hand and Flowers a knot of villagers said goodnight to one another. They dispersed along the lanes, singing in slurred voices. Their 'goodnights' rang between the hedges. The bar with its uncurtained window was blue with smoke; the landlord crossed and recrossed it, carrying tankards, behind him on the wall a great tarnished fish in a glass case.

From the cottages all along the village came blurred and muted wireless music. Some of the doors stood open to the scented night, revealing little pictures of interiors, fleeting and enchanting, those cottage rooms which Frances loved so dearly, with their ornaments, their coronation-mugs, their tabby cats. Night-scented stocks lined garden-paths, curled shells were arranged on window-sills, and on drawn blinds were printed the shadows of geraniums or a bird-cage shrouded for the night.

As she came near the cottage, she heard Frances

playing the piano. She went in through the back door, on her way gathering a row of Harry's napkins from the clothes-line. In the kitchen, she smoothed them and folded them at the table. They were sweet with the fragrance of washing that has hung out in the night air. She put them on the rack over the stove and sat down at the table, thinking of Liz, and unwilling for the moment to face the piano-playing in the other room. Hotchkiss sniffed at his plate of biscuit, found nothing new there, and lay down in a disheartened way on the doormat. Camilla watched him, her cheek in her hand, her mouth drooping.

The piano-playing stopped without her noticing and Frances came down the passage.

"What's wrong? Have you toothache?"

"No. Why do you ask?"

"You look dejected."

"Toothache isn't the only cause of dejection."

Frances went over to the sink. "What is the cause, then?" she asked, above the sound of water drumming into the kettle.

"I'm depressed about Liz."

"Life is never perfect for anyone."

"Arthur is so callous and self-important."

"And yet you would change places with her."

"I?"

"At any time."

"It wouldn't be so bad for me. I am less vulnerable than Liz."

"It is a good thing she is vulnerable."

"Even with life so imperfect?"

Frances spread her hands over the gas-ring. She was often cold nowadays and conscious of her age. Her hands were wrinkled and shiny, skin transparent over veins, nails sunk into the flesh. She turned them slowly over the flame. "Life persists in the vulnerable, the sensitive," she said. "*They* carry it on. The invulnerable, the too-heavily armoured perish. Fearful, ill-adapted, cumbersome, impersonal. Dinosaurs and men in tanks. But the stream of life flows differently, through the unarmed, the emotional, the highly personal . . ."

"You turn my anxiety about Liz into a disarmament conference," Camilla said.

"She has committed herself to that man. You were wrong at tea-time when you said she married Arthur, not the vicar. A man's work is twisted into the roots of his existence. His conscience is involved. He can't divide himself."

"On the contrary, Arthur seems to have a genius for cutting himself up into little pieces. He hands himself round among the ladies as if he were a plate of scones."

Frances made the tea and put cups on the table. She sat down and patted her thigh until Hotchkiss lumbered to his feet and padded over to her. Camilla poured out. "Oh, I'm tired!" she yawned.

"You see," Frances went on, "I know Liz so well. When she was a little girl, she was warm-hearted and impulsive, but quick to blame herself, quick to feel disappointment. She must absorb this disappointment

77

into her life like all the others. And you must let her."

"We only have *one* life."

"But there is room in it for everything. Like light, it contains all the colours. You are too fastidious."

"Too fastidious," Camilla repeated. She frowned as she drank her tea. "I don't any longer know what I am." She thought about her morning at the Griffin, her promise to return, the passion which had driven her out walking with Hotchkiss in the dark.

"We go on for years at a jog-trot," Frances said, "and then suddenly we are beset with doubts, the landscape darkens, we feel lost and alone, conscious all at once that we must grope our way forward for we cannot retrace our footsteps." She thought of her painting out in the shed, finished, awaiting Mr Beddoes.

She said: "You are the one I worry for, not Liz."

"I?" Camilla put her cup down, looking surprised.

"Because you never cry. Because you are so heavily armoured that if you get thrown, you'll never rise to your feet again without assistance."

"*You* shall assist me," Camilla said lightly. "I wonder what Liz is doing now."

She gathered up the cups and took them to the sink to wash them. Frances opened the door and let Hotchkiss out into the garden.

"I know," she said, standing on the step and looking at the sky. "When she was a child, her father was a bit heavy-handed with her. One of those dry, domineering men. There were often punishments of a formal cold-blooded kind. 'See me in the library after tea.' Not brutality. But talk, endless discussions about what would become of her character. She would stand there, fidgeting, while the words broke over her head. Disapproval is deadly poison, though; and she'd whiten with fatigue. And later, when I was brushing her hair, she'd begin to sob and go on and on even after she was in bed, not from remorse—heavens, no!—but from the feeling of coldness in those around her. I would go away, unable to help, and creep back a few minutes later with a warm drink. And there she'd be, her cheek turned to the pillow, beautifully asleep. And she'll be asleep now. She'll have quarrelled and cried and dropped off."

She leant into the darkness and whistled for Hotchkiss. "Whereas you," she added, speaking in a low voice in the quiet air, "will lie awake half the night, feeling isolated and bewildered. And you won't even know why."

Hotchkiss did not come and she took up a torch and went into the garden to look for him.

．　　　．　　　．　　　．

Richard was sitting in his room at the Griffin, writing in his diary.

'No mention for two days. Perhaps never again. But now these newspapers are a habit with me. I try to resist them, not to pick them up in the bar or the lounge, not to buy them, nor to go to the Reading Room at the Library. Because of the papers I see the thing differently now. What it really was, comes to me

79

only occasionally and with sudden freshness and vividness, as a shock. And now, alone in my room, in this stale, fusty, damnable, *dead* room, I try to concentrate on it, to face it again as a real thing. But it is like trying to live over an old embrace. When I was a youth, I would attempt to do that, to go through it all again when I was alone, from the first touch. But always it evaded me. And this evades me. All feeling, excitement, flies and vanishes. So I am always alone.'

His hands felt suddenly too cold to write, although it was a warm night; he was conscious of a chill, a kind of paralysis creeping over him; his thighs froze, his wrists were ice on the edge of the dressing-table at which he wrote. He put his pen down quietly and covered his face with his hands.

.   .   .   .

Camilla sat at her mirror late that night. Candles passed light across her face, put a little flicker in her eyes, a blueish shadow in her armpit as she brushed her hair.

"Alone!" she said suddenly out loud, and her eyelids wavered at the unexpected sound of her voice in the quiet room.

She shook her hair back and felt the sweep of it across her bare shoulders. The caress of it against her skin disquieted her, and, when she looked into the mirror again, excitement, even beauty, had changed her face. She leant forward into the picture of the room behind her—some of Liz's clothes lying untidily across her bed, the bed itself dinted from Liz's flung-down body, as, distracted and frustrated, she had lain there weeping, before she had suddenly roused herself, dried her eyes and begun to pack a few clothes, leaving a trail of disorder after her. In the picture framed by the mirror, Camilla's bed primly awaited her, the sheet neatly turned back, and for once she thought without disgust of the great rumpled beds in Frances's paintings which she had always looked at with fastidious, cold appraisal, but now longed for with the thought inherent in squeamish people that the sordid must always be truer to life than the agreeable.

The room was heaped with shadows and in the looking-glass was a dark background to the brilliance of her face, her throat and arms.

'The candlelight!' she thought, laying her brush down and leaning forward. 'By candlelight, all women have some sort of beauty!'

Her flesh was golden as an apricot; her hair, in contrast, looked tarnished and harshly bright.

'And there is no one to see,' she thought. 'In the day, I put on my tight face, my buttoned-up look. I hood my eyes, cover myself. But now, in my moment of beauty, there is no one to see me.'

She crossed her arms and slid down the ribbons of her nightgown from her shoulders. The picture in the mirror exasperated her. She remembered herself as a girl. The sharp white shoulders, the high bosom had so imperceptibly, yet so soon, assumed this heavy golden ripeness, and how much more abruptly would exchange maturity for old age. Not only the candlelight made her beauty seem precarious. In her youth, discipline, over-niceness had isolated her. Shyness, perhaps, or pride, had started her off in life with a false step, on the wrong foot. The first little mistake initiated all the others. So life gathered momentum and bore her away; she became colder, prouder, more deeply committed; and, because she had once refused, no more was offered. Her habit now was negative. A great effort would be needed to break out of this isolation, which was her punishment from life for having been too exclusive; she must be humbled, be shamed in her own eyes, scheme and dissemble for what she wanted or it would be too late.

'A hackneyed theme,' she told herself, her stubborn daytime face suddenly reflected back.

She drew her nightgown up over her shoulders again and began rapidly to plait her hair.

CHAPTER SIX

THE CHALK breaking through the short turf looked like the very bones of the earth. From this distance the town seemed embowered in trees; the hot bare streets had contracted, the few factories shrunk down under the canopy of leaves.

But the Saxon earthworks, which, seen from the bedroom windows of the Griffin, had so exactly crowned the hill-top, were now, at this closer range, merely an unevenness in the chalk, a great wavering ridge of broken hillside, too large for any shape to be discerned.

Out of breath from their climb, Richard and Camilla sat down on the rim of this saucer-like hill-top, looking back towards the town. The fine grass was studded with flat round thistles, rosetted, set deep in the turf like buttons in upholstery. The tiny hovering moths were the same colour as the harebells, and of the same transparency.

"You came here once before?" Camilla asked, turning over to lie on her belly on the grass, half-propped up on her elbows.

He sat looking down at her. He looked so steadily that her glance faltered and she turned awkwardly away, putting up a hand to her carefully-done but loosening hair, which she never could forget, and touched continually as if to reassure herself.

"I was a boy then," he said jerkily.

"I know."

"I came late one night, later than this. I sat down just about here and looked at the town."

"Why did you come?"

"I was lonely," he said crossly.

"But this would have made you lonelier." She turned to look at the great wavering line of chalk against the sky, the wide, empty landscape.

"I don't think so."

The colour was drawn out of the day. They had taken a long time to walk here, had been drinking before that. She shivered now, lying against the turf which had less warmth than her body.

"And when *you* came?" he said, leaning a little towards her.

"Oh, it was many times. With Liz. With books and bread-and-cheese." She said this flatly and hurriedly as if those happy days had no meaning. She blew a strand of hair out of her eyes and he leaned closer to her and smoothed it back from her forehead. She closed her eyes. Her heart beat against the ground; it was as if the sound of it went deep into the earth. She felt thistles pressing through her dress. He took some of the pins from the top of her head and a wing of hair dropped against her cheek.

"Please don't!" she said quickly, putting out her hand.

He leant right over her and loosened all her hair. She turned under him, her hands pressing his shoulders. Her hair had sprung out of its pins, as if it came down willingly. "Now forget it," he said. "I'll think about it. Not you." He leaned back, still looking at her, and then suddenly laughed.

She felt flustered and upset, tremulous with vexation. His behaviour toward her was intimate yet unadmiring, an easy kindness, which she had noticed in young men who are interested, not in women, but in other young men, and who imply that although the feminine secrets are laid bare to them, they will keep them and sustain them, but remain unmoved.

In the midst of her annoyance, he sighed sharply and turned his head restlessly to look at the sweep of the hillside, as if he were all at once overflowing with impatience.

"What is it?" she asked him.

His glance came back to her.

"I don't know. I suddenly feel I can't *stand* anything any more . . . the boredom—hopelessness. I miss the war."

Aghast, she said: "You were happier in the war?"

"Men always are."

"Oh, no!" Her denial was an entreaty, he thought.

"*My* sort of men are."

"But you said . . ."

"I said what?" he asked quickly.

"The first time I ever saw you, you told me that you'd

had enough, that it stopped just in time, your nerve was going."

"My nerve *has* gone," he said quietly.

"You need to be quiet and to rest," she suggested.

"No. I need excitement, I need . . ." he lifted his head, shut his eyes as if to concentrate, "things crashing against me, violence; the quiet will kill me."

"Why do you fear to be alone?"

"The war. The war made it impossible."

"But even in war you were alone, in your sort of job . . ."

"Oh yes," he agreed quickly. "Oh, I know." And then, "But it was somehow different."

"Why *have* you come here?" she asked in a low voice, her face almost touching the grass, as she spoke. She waited, but she guessed that she would never get an honest answer from him.

He groped and hesitated and gave up. "To write my book," he said.

"But you won't write it."

"Yes, I shall. When I write, something goes out of me. It runs down my arm and out through my fingers." He laughed. "It spills over on to the page. It quietens me."

"What sort of book will that make?" she asked.

He thought, not of the non-existent book, but of his diary, the way it drained the pain and frustration of the day out of him each night before he could sleep.

"I can't sleep," he said suddenly.

"No, I can see that. You've the heightened excitability of people who lie awake at night."

He was silent.

"What is really wrong with you?" she asked.

"I have never known," he said quietly.

"What happens?"

"It must be the same for everyone. I think we all *are* the same, only I fail to conceal it."

"The same in what way?"

"Isolated."

"There are other people always," she said. When she spoke to him, she looked into the grass, harebells brushed her forehead; but sometimes, as he was speaking, she flicked little glances at him.

"Other people," he interrupted. "Other people began with my mother, I suppose. But she was locked away in misery. When she took me in her arms, she was staring over my shoulder at her own unhappiness. I felt alone. And I *was* alone. My father. Well, he beat me. While he was doing that I was utterly alone. Pain put me outside the world. 'If only *I* were doing the thrashing!' I used to think. But nothing really quietens the heart."

"Heart?" she repeated, in a puzzled voice.

"And women. Love," he went on impatiently. "Where does it *lead* to, I wondered."

"Must it lead somewhere?" She smiled.

"For a few days it didn't need to. Then it would all seem like a play I was acting in. Been acting in a long time. A long run, and I knew all my lines too well and was stale and boring everyone. But most of all myself. Then I tried death."

"Death?"

"In the war," he said lightly. "I went up very close to it. My own and other people's. And there it was. Unlike all the other things, it never changed. It was always real. I seem to carry the thought of it about with me."

"You mustn't."

"Oh . . . I shan't . . . it's just that people are like doors. They all lead you into empty rooms. You pass through and are left with yourself. Only death goes through ahead of you."

"Life goes wherever you go . . ."

"No. Life is left behind. Little bits break off in your hands and you drop them. The rooms lead only to death," he insisted.

"They might lead to God," she suggested, but only to hold out some hope to him. She did not believe it herself.

A silence fell over him. For once, he did not take her up or interrupt. She tried to look at him, but could not. 'I must see his face,' she told herself. Her fingers tugged at and scattered the fine grass. Darkness was stealing up from the east and the earth seemed to reel over into shadow. She summoned all her will-power and sat up and looked straight at him. He was staring at her, and whatever she had expected was not there, for his face was expressionless.

The strangeness of her situation came over her with

88

her realisation of approaching darkness, the knowledge that she sat on this hillside, her hair down to her shoulders, quite out of the context of all the rest of her life. Ecstasy, she thought. She took the word to pieces and saw its true meaning. The first meanings of words go deeper, she understood, than any of their later meanings, which are fleshed-over and softened by convention and repetition. To go back to the beginnings of words is like imagining the skeletons of our friends.

'The same thing happened to us both,' she thought, 'but there's no logic about human beings. Both of us starved as children, but he (perhaps because he is a man) reacting to violence, inviting danger, attempting everything and everyone. While I am stiffening into an old maid, recoiling fastidiously from life. Closed, exclusive, self-contained, sarcastic.'

She found his steady gaze unendurable and wished that he would either talk or take her in his arms.

"We are the same," she said, and she looked down at the grass, embarrassed. "The same sort of childhood. Beaten and frustrated. Perhaps that sets us on one side."

"Beaten?" he repeated quickly.

"Not I. No. But frustrated."

"Tell me."

She shut her eyes and smiled, bringing it back.

"A dark Victorian house, muffled rooms, too many books. My brothers walking up and down *discussing*. Any subject, so long as it came nowhere near their hearts, or emotion or reality. Their dry voices, their pale faces; a man's world. They were all older than me. None of them married. I sat there as a child, reading a book, conforming exactly to their idea of what a little girl should be; precocious, sedate, trying to look like Alice in Wonderland. I accepted it all, their voices, the cerebral atmosphere; though I was being choked by it. My mother was proud of their intelligence, she catered to that masculine world, and upheld it, tiptoeing about, being a housekeeper. My father was only another son to her. Cambridge. Oh, God, the dryness of it, the superiority, the falseness. Right outside life as it is for most people. The visitors who called were only my brothers over again. Donnish, remote. Silly jokes, irritating mannerisms, respected eccentricities, no spontaneity. But worst of all, for *me*, nothing feminine. It was all exclusively male. No one talked about hats."

She turned to him and laughed. "So I grew up *unable* to talk about hats, thinking fashion unimportant and absurd and even shameful. Not abstract enough, you see. Then I met Liz. We went to a school in Switzerland together. She alone broke through the coldness I had gathered about me. She was impulsive and warm, went out after friends, could humble herself, never anticipated rebuffs as I did, didn't mind looking a fool. For the first time in my life I gossiped, I giggled, I confided, I talked about clothes, I threw away what my brothers would have called 'my personal code', which was only a rigid and preconceived set of rules to take the place of loving-kindness. I owe all that to Liz. She's capricious and not very wise. She laughs about men, and then loves them too easily. I had been brought up to respect them, but never to seek them. Why am I telling you all this?"

"Go on," he said.

"No, I must go home. It isn't that Liz was particularly happy as a child, but she was allowed to be loving. Her father was a pompous creature, her mother, whom she adored, died when she was twelve. She was overwhelmed by grief, but not distracted by it. You see, her mother had taught her to be loving, had kissed her and tucked her in for the night, leaving her secure in warmth. She left her like that when she died. I think children must be encouraged to love or they will close up. Or hate."

"Or love themselves too much," he said.

She agreed quickly. Had he, she wondered, spent his life studying his own reflection in a pool? Absorbed in himself, until no one else was any good? No longer seen, even; but crowded out by his own image.

When he stood up suddenly, she was piqued that she had not done so first. He stretched out his hand to her and, as she clasped it, drew her to her feet. She shivered, and he pulled her closer to him and into his arms and kissed her. His mouth was colder than her own. Then, very calmly, he put her away from him and looked at her.

'He stares at me so,' she thought, faltering and discouraged. As they began to walk down the hill she

lifted her eyes to the sky, which was bruised all over
with darkness. The harebells were colourless and pale
at their feet; and the earthworks behind them, a great
broken and menacing outline. Lights pricked the
valley and seemed to lie like blossoms on the branches
of the trees.

As she walked, she tried to control the deep, shaken
breaths which unsteadied her. Her body felt dragged
and hollowed with her longing for him to resume their
embrace and to complete it. Suddenly she was con-
founded by the realisation that all her self-protection
meant nothing to her; her pride, her over-niceness, her
front to the world, she had abandoned so easily and to a
stranger. Her motive at first—but she had forgotten it
already—had been to show-off to Liz, to deny her own
virginity, to punish her for the baby and all the
physical experience it symbolised.

She felt over-wrought, tired and ready to weep, as
she stumbled down the uneven hillside with him.
Neither of them spoke.

A stile led into a lane with high hedges. As he lifted
her down, she could faintly discern his face in the
darkness. His lips parted, as if he were about to speak,
his eyes slanted thoughtfully, and then he shrugged and
said nothing. They walked down the lane, and here
they were sheltered and the warmth of the day still
lingered between the hedgerows.

Presently he said: "I must of course see you again."

She said nothing, but she thought: 'I shall get over
this night somehow, for there will be others.'

"When shall I?" he was asking.

"Oh, my hair!" she cried. "I can never go home with my hair like this."

"It's quite dark."

"But Frances will see me."

"Who is Frances?"

She explained Frances hastily, for she had no part in this. He listened, but as soon as she had stopped he said: "*When* shall I see you?"

"I don't know."

"Think!"

"It depends on other people, on Liz and Frances. I'm not on my own. But I shall see you somehow. I will leave a message for you in the bar."

Mr Beddoes she suddenly remembered, and how on Sunday he would be at the Griffin, too. And in the morning Liz would come back. Her steps quickened, and the sad confusion left her: thoughts of the outside world drove it from her, as she had forced them to for years.

"You do promise?" he asked, looking straight ahead.

They passed under the railway-arch and, her voice suddenly echoing and metallic: "Yes, I promise," she said.

.   .   .   .

Richard went back to his room at the hotel and unlocked his diary from his suitcase. For a while, he sat staring at it and thinking, and then, as if he were controlled by the pen itself, he began to write, the words pouring out and slanting across the page. His face was

93

quite set. He wrote until his whole body was stiff and cramped. . . .

'. . . I am closer to her with words than I ever was with loving anybody, or hurting them, because her mind unlocks my mind. She takes away my loneliness and comforts me. She keeps me company, which is all I need now. She does not expect me to make love to her, as other women do. If I have only days left, or weeks, or nothing, I will never do anything to her, I will never again kiss her or lay a hand upon her. For I think God has sent her to me to help me to die, to give me a chance. It was never that I didn't believe in Him, but He didn't believe in me. When she said that at the end there is God I felt that what she said was right. She steadies me and listens to me and I will never harm her or lay a hand upon her. This is real closeness. When people touch one another, they are most of all alone. We are all like icebergs; underneath where the greater parts are hidden it is dark and unreachable. That hidden part is our secret thoughts and our childhood, our dreams and our fears. She shall accompany me there. And because she is the last thing that will ever happen to me, it shall be different from all that went before. More important. I will make it different and perfect. And I shall never touch her or harm her or lay hands upon her . . .'

His face was tired. He fell into endless repetitions, his pen travelling fast, from left to right across the page, and the light rained down over him, harsh and bright from under the torn silk shade.

CHAPTER SEVEN

IT WAS Mrs Parsons's day. She came up from the village
on Saturdays to do the rough, her white hair bound in a
mauve turban, her eyes all the time narrowed against
her cigarette smoke. She loved praise and constantly
invited it, taking Frances to inspect her work, the
polished furniture, the turned-out bedroom.

"Now, madam dear," she would say, halting in the
doorway, linking her arm with Frances's as no one else
would dare to do, "just tell me please if you can find a
cobweb. Look anywhere you like, dear; I defy you to
find one." Frances could not. "I like to see everything
neat and clean," she would say. This was true. She
abhorred untidiness or Bohemianism.

Mrs Parsons disliked Camilla, although Camilla was
at great pains to be pleasant. "Each to their own walk
of life," she would say, meaning she mistrusted
Camilla's, which she had summed up (from the books
on the bedside-table) as a sterile London life—politics,
meetings, interference with other people's affairs.
Then, too, people in London seemed not to marry as
they did in the country. The village girls married in
their early twenties, Mrs Parsons herself at the age of
eighteen. In London, women in their thirties un-

concernedly set up house on their own, as if they had all their lives before them in which to find husbands and bear children.

Frances was accepted in the village. She held a place in the community, or rather on the fringe of it, which would have distressed and puzzled her if she had known. Living there, alone in her cottage, just outside the village, they thought of her as an eccentric, as one of those local characters which all such rural societies encompass—the village idiot, the gossiping post-mistress, the absent-minded vicar and, thus—Frances herself—the slightly cracked old maid with her bee-keeping and her sketching. Two hundred years earlier she might have been the local witch.

So intent was she on being a normal elderly woman, so much trouble did she take, that she would always rather be praised for her crab-apple jelly than her painting, for the first was a marvel in her, the other natural to her and inevitable. Detesting the artists she had met and the milieu in which they usually worked she painted at set hours and did the washing-up first, remembering always Flaubert's advice to artists— "Be regular and ordinary in your life, like a bourgeois, so that you can be violent and original in your works." She would have been distressed beyond measure and bewildered if she had known how *extra*-ordinary the villagers thought her, or how Mrs Parsons on Saturday nights at the pub, spoke of her as 'my poor dear lady', pitying her, or told stories of her little mad kindnesses, her presents of money, of dried herbs, of cowslip wine, of jars of honey, of advice: how she had searched the snowy fields one winter's night, hearing a rabbit crying in a trap, and had given her dinner to the dog when she was short of meat and eaten bread and marmalade herself. These actions, so natural to Frances that she would never have believed that ordinary people could behave otherwise, were enough to set the stories circulating, but she remained quite ignorant of them, and when Mrs Parsons took her arm, she thought it a gesture of simple kindness, not protection.

This morning, Mrs Parsons had brought something in with her as well as her basket with its rolled-up pinafore. Tragedy, Frances thought it was. Camilla said she was sullen, that she would give her notice before the day was out. Yet it was grief that made Mrs Parsons carry herself so stiffly, behave so impeccably. Usually loose in her speech, this morning she discriminated with her words; her conversation became portentous with grandeur, the construction of her sentences so involved that they could not be rounded off, but hung in mid-air, abandoned, until Frances was confused and began to shout as if she were talking to a foreigner and presently gave it up.

At eleven o'clock, loosened perhaps by tea, Mrs Parsons broke off and said: "Oh, madam dear," and put her handkerchief to her eyes. Her language, when she could resume, was simple again and Anglo-Saxon. For the great Latinised sentences were useless to describe or deal with emotion—or shame, as it turned out to be.

How immediately, Frances thought, we leap to obvious conclusions, and how right we always are.

"It's Euniss again, madam."

At home, this daughter was sometimes affectionately nick-named Eunicey, a pronunciation of Camilla's which was a family joke and put them all into agonies of suppressed laughter.

"Yes, I thought it would be that," Frances said. She was naturally not so distressed as a mother would be; but, on the other hand, did not regard the situation, though hackneyed, as either comic or shameful. Once before, Euniss had been in trouble, but there had been a miscarriage, especially Frances thought, of justice.

Camilla got up and left the room. This act of sensibility was at once misjudged and would not be forgiven. She made the mistake always of thinking people would like what she herself liked; she put herself too much in other people's places, instead of allowing them to stay there themselves.

Upstairs, feeling vaguely ruffled, she walked about her bedroom. From below, in the kitchen, came the sound of Mrs Parsons's laughter, of her rich and Guinness-lined voice.

Frances was busy displaying a natural and looked-for curiosity, which Camilla would have concealed. She asked all the questions which Mrs Parsons required her to ask, the practical questions such as when and who and what next. Mrs Parsons herself had brightened. In the discussion of trouble lies the comfort for it, and of this she sensibly made the most she could.

"She thinks it was the man who came to read the meter."

"She *thinks*!" Frances protested.

"Well, of course, it could be Ernie." Ernie was her fiancé, but his claims seemed less than those of a casual stranger.

"It would be better if it were Ernie," Frances suggested.

"In many ways, no doubt. But Ernie is only a labourer, the other has a profession at the back of him."

"But will he recognise his responsibility?"

"It's getting hold of him in the first place, madam."

"Poor Euniss. Yes, of course."

"We can't afford to wait until the next half-yearly reading."

"What is his name?"

"She remembers him as mentioning either Roy or Ken. Quite a short name, she says. She was to have met him the next evening, only it rained. Whether he turned up himself or not we don't know. As things have happened, it would have been better for her to have slipped on her mac and gone, only Ernie came round after tea and that put the tin lid on it together with the rain. We had a listen to the wireless instead."

"What would Ernie say to all this?"

"He wouldn't stand for it, madam. And quite right too he *is* so touchy. Her dad won't stand for it, either, forgetting how he carried on hisself."

"Do you mean he'll turn her out?" Frances asked, her

knowledge of such situations based on Edwardian melodrama.

Mrs Parsons was astonished. "Turn his own daughter out, madam! I'd like to see him try. Whatever do you think they'd say at the Flowers if I let him behave like that? And where, poor girl, could she go?"

Seeming not to have heard of the streets of London, her imagination travelled no farther than the pub and her own position in the Ladies' Darts Team. "No, when I said he wouldn't stand for it, I meant he'd carry on, the same as what Ernie will."

"Poor Euniss," Frances said again, and with the prospect of saying it much more.

"Yes. None of us are saints, madam, but some of us are luckier than the rest."

She took cigarettes and matches from her skirt pocket and lit up. "Well, the work's gone to the wall this morning and no mistake," she said, rinsing cups at the sink.

Liz came past the kitchen-window with Arthur, carrying the baby between them in a Moses basket. She opened the kitchen door and put her finger to her lips. Harry slept beautifully, his mouth parted, his veined eyelids still.

Arthur tiptoed away to fetch the luggage from the car. When he had gone, Mrs Parsons whispered to Frances: "Say nothing for the time being, madam, him being a parson."

"Say nothing about what?" Liz asked.

"Tell you later," Mrs Parsons promised gaily. She

had wrought a great change upon herself since her arrival. Stimulated by company, drama quickened the tempo of her life, lifted her up, and made this a red-letter day.

Liz went creaking upstairs with the cradle and put Harry into his little room among the stacked canvases. Camilla was dusting their dressing-table.

"What's going on downstairs that must be kept from Arthur?" Liz enquired.

"Hallo Liz. It's Euniss Parsons, I expect."

"I thought it must be something like that. It is usually sex that clergymen mustn't hear about. Poor Euniss. How far gone is she?"

"How far gone! No, really Liz! I'm not going to talk that sort of language to you. You'll be telling me next about what a bad time you had with Harry."

"Well, so I did. It's that Ernie, I suppose."

"I don't know who that Ernie is."

"The lad at the farm. Brings the milk. She's engaged to him."

"Well, perhaps it is. It's their own affair and I don't know them and can't be interested."

She polished the mirror furiously and Liz saw her reddened face reflected in it. She said meekly, changing the subject: "I had a nice time at home after all."

"I'm glad."

"What have *you* been doing?"

Camilla's hand slowed over the mirror and then dropped to her side. For a second, she seemed to relax, her lips formed the word 'I'; but it was as if her mind were too clouded to form a sentence. Then she said crisply: "I never question *you* about your comings and goings."

"That's the trouble with you. You wait for people to tell you things. So they feel you don't care."

"It isn't that. You are like a newly-married wife with your anxious curiosity . . . 'and *then* what did you do?' . . . 'and after *that* where did you go?' You must leave me alone."

"You don't want to be left alone. You want to tell me, but you are too much afraid of behaving badly; or rather, behaving like other people. And you will tear that duster to shreds."

Liz sat down on her bed and began to strip off her stockings. "I know you went out with that man," she continued. "I guessed you were going to. You were half-relieved to send me off with Arthur, so that you could."

"You try to be so perceptive, but you are quite wrong."

"You *did* go out with him."

Camilla sat down at the dressing-table. She felt an icy paralysis creeping over her, even her lips seemed frozen.

"Do you know where my sandals are?" Liz asked.

"The bottom shelf of the cupboard."

Liz pottered about the room and Camilla sat staring in front of her at the dressing-table. When Liz was ready to go down, she went over and put her hand on Camilla's shoulder, rather timidly, because she was shy of touching her.

"Frances is furious with me," Camilla said. "Yes, I did go. And I came back very late. She had waited up for me, and I believe thought I was drunk. Which I was not."

"You are not a girl in your 'teens, Frances forgets."

"But my behaviour as a guest!"

"Remember her conventionality and her genteel ways are an exaggeration she goes in for deliberately, a brake she imposes on herself, because of her painting, and perhaps because she fears she might so easily become quite otherwise."

"I know all that. Heaven knows, I keep telling myself. But by *any* standards . . ."

"It isn't this which has upset you."

"Don't ask me any women's questions," Camilla said quickly.

"No, I won't. But not because I don't care."

"From the first I thought this holiday would be terribly different from all the rest."

"Go home then! Come home with me! Let us go together. I can tell Frances that Arthur needs me, as indeed he does."

"No, I have to stay."

"But why?"

"I just do have to."

"There is some mystery. He is not your sort of man." Liz walked about the room disarranging things.

"Arthur is not *your* sort of man," Camilla said sharply. Then she sighed, as if she were unbearably

103

oppressed. She stood up and looked out of the window. "Yes, there is some mystery," she admitted. "I don't understand either."

"Perhaps if we were not so *clever* we'd understand," Liz laughed.

They went downstairs. Arthur was drinking rhubarb wine in the parlour. His life was full of such little duties and, since he was obliged to drink the wine, he did so always with this good grace; with relish, even. He could afford to seem over-occupied with little worldly pleasures. He seemed to display this minor trait in such a way that it indicated more clearly the great spiritual side of his nature lying in the shadow.

He and Frances were studying the cacti, half-empty glasses in their hands.

"Stockings off already?" he said, turning as Liz and Camilla came in. Then he added to Frances, as she began to fill two more glasses: "She runs in as fast as she can, and goes round and round like a cat, until she is comfortable. As if this were her real home."

"Cups of tea, glasses of wine!" Camilla said. "One way and another it *is* being a morning."

"Push Liz Barrett off the sofa, Arthur, and sit down," his wife said.

He did not in time stop himself from glancing round.

"It is an absurd game they play," Frances apologised. "Did you enjoy your trip, Elizabeth?"

"Yes, I did, thank you."

"You sound so surprised," Arthur said.

"Well . . . I didn't know people would be so nice to me . . ."

"People are always nice to one if one does one's duty," Frances said.

"Frances, don't be so superb!" Camilla protested. "And you could not have been more tactless to Arthur."

"I am afraid Camilla is right," he said sadly, but sad rather because he was forced to agree with her than for his tragic conclusion about humanity. "We are persecuted for doing our duty more often than not."

"Then I must thank my stars it went off as well as it did for me," said Liz. "Are *you* much persecuted then, Arthur?"

"Perhaps I am," he said, smiling mysteriously, and he put his hand under her hair and clasped the back of her neck. "Darling!" he added. A little awkwardness fell over them all.

In the kitchen, Mrs Parsons, not quite spontaneously, sang 'Rock of Ages Cleft For Me', her voice loud and serious; as if this were the last hymn before the boat went down.

"Well, somebody is happy," Arthur remarked. He unclasped Liz and stood up from the arm of her chair. "I must go. Be safe and happy, pet." He saw Camilla look scornfully into her wine-glass.

"When shall we see you again?" Frances asked, with a vague attempt at hospitality. "You must come to tea."

"Yes, I should like to come to have tea with my wife. And, of course, with you."

Liz went out with him and at the door he looked back and said: "You would have been proud of her, Miss Rutherford. She managed very well. Very naturally. Just as I knew she would."

"Natural behaviour always goes down well," Frances said happily.

"I wish He would *let* her to His Bosom flee," Camilla said restlessly, for in the kitchen, the hymns continued above, appropriately, the sound of running water. She watched Liz and Arthur going down the path. At the gate, they kissed.

"Frances!" Camilla began, turning quickly away from the window. But Frances had gone back to her painting.

Mrs Parsons came in to collect the glasses. "That's a lovely wine madam makes," she said, lingering by the decanter. She replaced the stopper sadly. "As fresh as port," she added. "Though I'm not a great wine-drinker." She debated the point within herself. "No. I shouldn't say I was a great wine-drinker," she concluded.

"What's all this about Euniss?" Liz asked briskly, coming back into the room.

Mrs Parsons set the tray down again.

"I'm afraid Euniss has been a naughty girl," she said sternly.

"Would you like a glass of this stuff?" Liz asked her.

Mrs Parsons sat down humbly before the rhubarb wine, as if it could not be taken standing up.

"I expect you're very worried," Liz suggested.

"Here's good health to you, madam, and many thanks! Yes, I am worried and there's no mistake. She's a very wilful girl and always was. Never one to sit down quiet with a book, but restless and on the go the minute she gets indoors. Glance at the paper, peck at her supper, fiddle with her hair, turn on the wireless and then don't listen to it. This is lovely and warming. Yes, she's been engaged to Ernie the twelve-month now and I've never once seen her bring out a piece of fancywork or crocher a mat, not like we did when we were girls, for our bottom drawers. And she's funny with Ernie, very sarky sometimes the way she answers him back—'So what?' and 'You don't say!' and all that. He takes it too meek and mild. Her dad would have knocked me down, if I'd spoken like that to him."

"Perhaps the sooner she marries Ernie the better," Liz suggested optimistically.

"If he will. Now," Mrs Parsons said simply. She stared in front of her, her hands folded on her apron.

"But it *is* Ernie who . . .?"

"It's a possibility, madam, certainly."

Mrs Parsons stood up and pushed her chair under the table again. "Yes, I wonder what will become of the girl. I lie awake at night sometimes and wonder. Well, thank you, that was lovely. I enjoyed that."

"If there's anything I could do," Liz began. "I, or my husband . . ."

She was suddenly, as she linked Arthur's name

with her own, conscious of Camilla standing very quiet and aloof by the window.

"Oh, madam, I hope you'd say nothing to the gentleman. Please, if you don't mind, it's just between ourselves and mustn't go no further. But thank you for the wine."

When she had gone, Liz replaced the stopper in the decanter, and stood there, very still; the sunlight coming in diamonds through the lace curtains chequered and broke up the picture of her, flashed in the wine, spilt over the carpet and revealed the tawny wreaths lying on the pink. Gold dust drifted upwards through the imprisoned sunshine, but nothing else moved until Camilla broke the moment with a sudden gesture and harsh words.

"That sycophantic old fool!" she cried. "I wonder why she doesn't curtsy as well."

"Mrs Parsons? It springs from a wish to be kind. And she doesn't deserve to be called a fool. Not that word; which seems to me a sort of blasphemy."

"Your trip home seems to have given your marriage a new lease of life."

"It was time it had one."

"So you are going to settle down?"

"I was always going to settle down."

"For all the rest of your life?"

"I expect so," Liz said calmly. "Marriage is nothing if it is not going in and slamming the door. It makes a pattern and provides a frame."

"And a fine array of metaphors. Why not say what you

think—that you have fallen again under Arthur's spell and mean to stay enchanted—for Harry's sake, perhaps."

"That would be a metaphor, too," Liz suggested.

"You still—care for Arthur?"

She closed her hand over the barbed cushion of a cactus and shut her eyes.

"I like *him* to care for *me*," said Liz.

"And does he?"

Liz stirred, like a cat that is suddenly filled with uneasiness and disquiet. She looked across at Camilla, who stood with her back to the light.

"You hope he doesn't," she said slowly. Her voice was dull and quiet and did not express the enormity of this discovery, nor match her unsteady breathing, nor her frown. "You hate him so much, you hope he doesn't care for me."

The sunlight fell all over her; her face, with its frown, its fear, its pleading, even tears, laid open to Camilla. But Camilla would not look at her, even though she stood in the safety of her own shadow. The palm of her hand still pressed into the cactus-plant—for only sharp discomfort could stop her trembling—and her foot tapped out on the carpet the rhythm beating in her forehead, an insistent rhythm which swelled and dominated her, until it seemed to be the rhythm of the room itself, of all the hot summer days, and this alien world she now sensed lying about her, and into which she had stepped with her hands spread out as if she were blindfold—so suddenly, so unreadily, and so late.

Frances was working in her studio, stretching a canvas. The key was turned in its lock; and, shut in and private, she had changed. She had put off her governessy ways. The need to snatch at those hastily-chosen platitudes about life and behaviour was gone; so she relaxed and, as she relaxed, she became mannish; she whistled, even; trod about heavily, and her hands —she wore her father's signet-ring—were like a man's hands as she worked.

The old-maidishness was something she assumed, but she thought it could be done artlessly and simply, like tying a velvet ribbon round her throat—she put it on and off, but never lived the part, so the insipid, flat remarks were made, conventions were tremendously respected, and Arthur, an important symbol in her fantasy, especially venerated.

Alone, with the door locked, she felt safe to paint and to be herself. To her, work was a loosening of will, a throwing down of defences. Sitting back, utterly malleable, her personality discarded like a snake's skin, she became receptive, and so creative. Unperceived lights now struck her, and her concentration could lift each leaf from its fellows, separate and halo every flower. To be interrupted was like having a foot tread down layers of ice in her breast, painful and humiliating, but destructive above all; for the vision, or the illusion, would hasten away.

As a child, beguiled, enchanted, she had drifted from one object to another—the little treasures of childhood, the veined pebbles, raindrops lying like mercury on hairy leaves, shells, whorled fossils, waxen petals—holding them in her hands, not knowing yet what use to make of them, but pained by her inadequacy.

Painting lessons did not teach her. She drew well, with pleasure. The pictures of apples and flowers and check dusters resembled the apples and flowers and check dusters; the resemblance was like one person dressing-up in another's clothes, an outward, visible likeness was achieved, but the inward, invisible transference was not made.

Then, one day, when she was a young woman, she suddenly, and as if by chance, related her talent to her genius. She cast away the dressing-up clothes and willed herself into what she painted. She threw away her personality and it changed. The nervous effort was extreme, for the difference was the distance between charades at parties and Sarah Bernhardt as Phèdre.

The apples, the dusters, though, seemed (her teachers thought) not so much like apples and dusters as formerly. "She has been praised too much," they decided, "and has stopped trying. Some talent comes early and leaves early and here is a good example. How glossy her fruit was once; how beautifully the high-lights shone like little windows on every grape. You could eat them almost. And that piece of lace on the table; how painstaking she used to be."

But their verdict did not matter. She could go on looking at things, and now knew, not frustration, but precisely what she should do with what she saw. This happiness overrode the disadvantage of her gift.

She was robust physically and mentally. She worked for her living. Her life was sparse and lonely. In the middle of a party, silence would come down in her like a shutter, the need to be alone; so she gave up going into company. She saved her money and she bided her time, and painted.

Then, when she felt near the end of her work, the world changed; or, as she herself thought, she peeped out from the briers of her imagination for the first time. The apple, the rose, were still the same, but violence swung about them. She felt ashamed of her preoccupation with stillness, with her aerial flowers, her delicate colours, her femininity. She was tempted outside her range as an artist, and for the first time painted from an inner darkness, groping and undisciplined, as if in an act of relief from her own turmoil.

These four paintings now stood against the wall, awaiting Mr Beddoes, her early patron, her unknown correspondent. She feared the moment of turning them before his eyes; for only Liz had ever seen them, and Liz she still thought of as a child.

Now, the canvas was stretched and tacked. She lifted it to the easel and sat down and smiled. It was as if the other paintings were sent into the corner, and stood there, sulky and unsuccessful; while here she was alone with her vision again.

'My last painting, perhaps,' she thought. 'The first stroke for the last time.'

But she could not make it. She sat, gently rubbing

her shoulder and smiling at the canvas. Pain ran down her arm and spread out its clinging fingers like ivy on a tree.

Nursing her elbow, she felt calm and confident: for if not today, there would be tomorrow; and with that prevailing promise, she had always worked.

Painting was her dearest pleasure; she did not look for the chance of it every day. It had never been thus, and never would be now.

CHAPTER EIGHT

"I THINK he looks *pinched*," Liz said.

They bent over the baby and observed him closely. He smelt of milk. Each time he seemed about to drop into a sleep, into a steadier rhythm of breathing, his violet eyelids would fly up suddenly, and he would stir on his pillow, or draw his legs to his stomach. He whimpered a little and sometimes turned his fist at his mouth, hungrily.

"His toes are full of fluff from the blanket," said Camilla.

"Yes, he's restless. He's in pain." And Liz at once decided he would die. She put the palm of her hand on his brow. "I wish Arthur were here."

"The child's teething," Frances said, looking in at the door.

"But he hasn't dropped off the whole afternoon."

"It's the heat," Camilla said. "We shall have to go, Liz."

"You must be there in time for Morland," Frances said.

"Morland!" Camilla cried delightedly.

"Yes, how lovely!" Liz said vaguely, looking at her son.

"Why did you keep the Morland part from us?"
Camilla asked Frances, leaning over the banisters to
watch her go downstairs.

"The name didn't arise. What is so strange about
it?"

"Nothing. Many men must be called Morland
Beddoes. I am only glad that he sounds so ordinary."

"I shan't come," Liz said.

"But you must!"

"I can't leave Harry."

"And I can't go to meet this man all on my own."

They would not exchange glances. They were lost to
one another. A no-man's-land lay between them now, a
terrain of unshared experience. The long years of
intimacy, the letters spilling over untidily from page to
page, the perfect matching of mood and humour, the
exactly-followed translations from deep sincerity to
mockery or innuendo, now buckled up and came to a
standstill. Only embarrassment stirred them.

Camilla set off alone on what would once have been a
shared delight, a little adventure woven into the fabric
of their common life; and Liz stayed behind, her baby
laid against her shoulder while she paced the room,
patting his back till his eyes goggled and the little soft
belches ran up one after the other, dribble hanging
from his chin.

'If only I were at home!' Liz thought. 'If only
Arthur were with me now.'

She stood for a moment by the window to smile goodbye to Camilla as she set out with Hotchkiss to meet

Mr Beddoes. The smile was all ready, but Camilla did not turn. She latched the gate with careful attention, without raising her head. Only Hotchkiss rolled a bloodshot eye towards her, slouching off along the hot road.

Liz sighed and turned back to pace the shadowed room with its plants and its plush and its ticking clock.

The early evening approached them. With Harry still sicking up his last meal, poor Liz prepared him for his next. His little chafed behind was lifted from the steaming napkins. As she sponged and powdered, her tears dropped all over him. Mr Beddoes was no adventure. He was unreal, was nothing. Only Arthur was real to her now, and what she took to be their dying son. She prayed as she opened her blouse. The tears rolled out of the corners of her eyes. She imagined Arthur going briskly from vicarage to church, in the scented evening, nodding to right and left, wearing his secret, his mysterious smile. The shadow of the church doorway would descend sharply like the guillotine, severing the quivering, radiant evening—and Arthur, shaking off the sunlight, would think of his sermon, ready to flay—who would it be this evening? Liz wondered.

'Whom will he lay about this time?' his parishioners also wondered, as they stepped along under the hubbub of the church bells, the exciting clangour and chaos of them. 'Who will it be this evening? The lapsed communicants or the T.U.C.? The Pharisees or the Labour Party?' Going primly up the path to the

116

West door, prayer-books in gloved hands, they were game for anything.

Now—a very different sound—the bell above the Methodist Chapel began to tilt to and fro. Clang, clang, it nagged. No tumult in the air, no flock of sound.

Liz took the baby's leech-like mouth from one breast and settled it to the other. The tears had dried stiffly on her face.

Upstairs, Frances put the corner of her handkerchief to a bottle of lavender-water. Her face was brown silk in the mirror. She put up her hand and smoothed her hair from the parting—an old woman's gesture.

The bell had stopped. An elephantine wheezing from the harmonium now followed, and a little later a skein of women's voices broke away, soaring, quivering up tremulously, but presently militantly and at last shrilly. Fight the Good Fight With All Thy Might.

Arthur would have winced, and smiled his secret, his mysterious smile.

.   .   .   .

"He will recognise the dog," Frances had said.

"Or I could wear a red carnation," Camilla suggested quickly.

"No need. Hotchkiss will be better for the walk, and I once described him in a letter."

'We think every word we put on paper is remembered for all time,' Camilla thought now, going along the Sunday-evening streets. 'As if they are more permanent than the spoken word. As if people nowadays tie them up in packets instead of dropping them page by page upon the fire. But sometimes there *are* letters which are like sheet-anchors to us, whatever sheet-anchors may be; they give depth and stability . . . we take them out and re-read them in trains, in buses, in the fish-queue, and last of all at night so that we sleep on their words. Crumb by crumb we taste them, until they begin to mean more than they were ever intended to mean. Mr Beddoes and Frances. Were their letters like that for one another; better than meeting, because a truer intimacy, each dipping—as it were—a little jug into the flowing-away past, arresting a moment here, a moment there, for the other's delight and understanding.'

She and Liz had always written thus, holding lighted candles to their lives, so that the other might see. 'It is the only thing,' she thought—but she glanced with scorn at the young people strolling the streets—'the only thing to make life worth living: human relationships. For our lives run into a loneliness which is like a dark grotto. Fearing to be solitary, we hold aloft a wavering light to tempt our friends into the darkness. "Look! It is thus!" we cry. The light falls not impartially, but directed by us, often unskilfully, so that cracks and fissures and grotesque shadows are inadvertently displayed. And in this clumsy illumination "It is thus! It is thus!" we plead, and "Thus is thus," the echoes go flying back over our shoulders. Our friends assent, but with their eyes perhaps on those uncovered cracks and fissures. They are never at our sides for long. And the wonder is that they should follow us at all.'

Oppressed by the staleness of this English Sunday evening, she felt a deadness about her and sadness in her heart so that she walked wretchedly, blindly, on past spiked railings, lace curtains, Montpelier House, Kitchener Villas, the rows of houses along which she and Liz once played their game of Aspidistra Tennis, scoring points for the plant-pots in the windows. 'Yes, the wonder is that our friends should follow us at all,' she thought, 'that there is ever anything but loneliness, like my life ahead next term, the set hours, the familiar framework of days, bicycling to and fro, the autumn leaves lying in the gutter, and then another winter, the evenings by the gas-fire in the bed-sitting-room, the concerts at the school, the lectures, the talks by missionaries, by elderly bird-watchers; the staff-room cups of tea; the little quarrels; the touchiness of one, the tactlessness of another; the betrothed games-mistress walking immune to it all as if bathed in a miraculous golden light; the little glances, the little edge to the voice. For women must not be left alone together. They betray one another for men. At a man's look, they drop the work in their hands, they turn their eyes away from their companions; his telephone-call can cancel all the rest, however late it comes!'

And now the houses were gone; shops took their place and on the Market Square, the Salvation Army band began to play. The bus queues watched apathetically, waiting to go out for the evening into the ripe countryside, or taking the children back home from tea with Granny in the town.

At this early hour, the young men walked together, or leant in groups against the cemetery railings, to watch the girls going by in couples, wearing pale frocks, net gloves, their hair pinned up elaborately at the front-room mirror and reflected now (they saw) in the blank shop-windows.

In the shops where no blinds were drawn, how static and remote the goods lay in the windows, as if touched by a wand and never to be moved again; and the pubs, too, so closed and so silent, as though deep in each beery fastness the landlord lay down on his bed to doze for ever, and opening-time would never come.

Opening-time would never come, the youths thought, lolling against the brawn-like marble or the green tiles below the scrolled and frosted windows, the sun warm on their foreheads.

The station held its spiked canopy out over the market-square and, stepping beneath it, shadow cool on her arms, Camilla fell suddenly apprehensive. For soon the train would come; it brought Mr Beddoes towards her, not any longer a disembodied joke, but flesh and blood, she thought. She tried to divest her mind of its comic picture, to be ready to make some effort, with thoughts and with words, and to prepare herself to encounter another personality to whom she would herself stand as a person.

The clock's hand jerked round, gold ran along the

railway lines, the groups of people stood motionless, waiting. Hotchkiss nosed at crates and wicker-baskets, turned his rather rheumy eyes with sly guilt as Camilla tugged him away.

'The train will never come,' she suddenly decided, gazing at the fixed signal and beyond it a glimpse of the Clumps rising above the valley, and the great broken crown of earth encircling them.

She sat down on a seat. Memory swerving in her forced her to shut her eyes. She could breathe the very air up there, the warm and herby smell; see the tiny starry flowers and the spongy turf, the butterflies; and feel the close, rosetted thistles against her thighs.

The signal fell with a sickening clatter, as if sharply dividing life and death. Everyone but Camilla seemed to move on the platform, some touched their luggage in readiness.

'That last time,' she thought, 'I was sure that I could never see railway-lines again without horror, watch a train approaching without associations of dread and apprehension. Yet I can. It is simply not the same thing. A different time, a different place, nothing the same. People say "I never hear that song without tears springing to my eyes," or "My heart turns over at the scent of arum-lilies; since Albert's funeral I couldn't have them in the house." But it is the truth twisted into the pattern we feel it should have; for the pattern has immortality woven into it, and our own importance in the world.'

The train came curving into sight along the gold

lines, its plume of smoke pearly in the sun, decorous as court-feathers, nodding in the still evening.

At first she thought it would never stop. It would continue to rush through the station, bearing Mr Beddoes with it, thin, irritable man that he would be, petulant old-maidish, self-infatuated, fastidious. Yes, she imagined him clearly, the sort of middle-aged man who buys pictures, who collects perhaps jade, or eighteenth-century fans, or Greek epitaphs, or Siamese cats, and hopes by doing so to enhance his own personality, who skims what little luxury is left from this evened-out England, finds still a little corner in which to gourmandise; a shirt-maker tucked away here, a place for brandy there (the train miraculously changed its rhythm and began to slow in beside the platform), his film-directing, Camilla thought, the only concession he makes to nowadays; for in these times, the middle-aged men with all day in which to go up and down the Bond Street galleries are few and far between. "Oh, I am a farmer now," they say with affected pride, at parties, or "I direct absurd films," or "I sell houses to people." Amazement and indignation lie under the words, for the old ties bind still, they will last one generation more. "Although we lend glamour to farming, to film-directing, to house-selling" they seem to say, "the wonder is that we are not spending the morning in Bond Street, sitting before a Vermeer in the back room, the old man awaiting our decision (which we shall not make until after luncheon); or descending into a cellar, where books are locked in safes, to turn the stained dark pages of a first edition copy of *Tristram Shandy*." Something has moved out of focus for them. What was so right, so admirable, has become dreadfully wrong. They blame (Camilla had heard so often) those who have less, that they themselves have not more.

She was glad about the shabby room at the Griffin, and the brawn and beetroot Mr Beddoes would surely get every evening for dinner.

She sat very still on the seat. 'I am middle-class,' she wished to declare. 'Middle-class women do not buy pictures; only prints of Van Gogh's Sunflowers to hang in their bed-sitting-rooms.'

Each traveller who emerged from the train seemed to have been miraculously brought to the end of his journey, but, even so, Mr Beddoes was more than could be expected, *he* would never untangle himself from the people spilling out over the platform to come certainly and with recognition towards the sleeping Hotchkiss.

One second the crowds clot and mingle on the platform; but, in the next instant, almost, they have sorted themselves out, the stream dwindles, the carriage doors are slammed, and if the one we seek is not there, he will not come.

'He will not come,' Camilla thought, immensely relieved.

No foreign-labelled luggage was handed out, no commotion was caused by suddenly obsequious porters, and soon there was left on the platform only a rather untidy, rather plump man, with a tie flying away in two ends and a rain-coat over his arm.

He came slowly but very certainly towards Camilla, his eyes upon Hotchkiss; for it was as Frances had said, and every word of all her letters he had remembered.

CHAPTER NINE

MORLAND BEDDOES was not in the least self-infatuated. He loved himself only as much as self-respect required, and the reason why he saw himself so clearly was that he looked not often, but suddenly, so catching himself unawares.

A perception he had, and kindness, caused his friends to run to him when they were troubled, for they were convinced of his absorption in their lives and could be sure that he would not judge them. In this way, his private life was continually impinged upon by distracted people. His sofa was not his own. Always, some man sat gloomily upon it, staring into a whisky and soda, waiting to unburden himself; or a slip of a girl would kick her shoes off, curl round among the cushions and weep, her hair over her face as a protection. The way he attracted wretchedness disturbed him, for no one ever came to him with good news.

He offered no advice, he took no sides, his flow of sympathetic phrases had dried up long ago and was reduced to murmurings. It must have been, he thought, like unbosoming oneself to a wood-pigeon. But still he listened, he offered brandy if need be, he slept on the floor while others occupied his bed, and often, weary from a day's work, would be brewing tea at two in the morning.

Always, human nature was displayed before him as a dishevelled thing; even in his film work he saw that poise was something put on and taken off like a cloak, never assumed for long; the cool-tempered, the suave, came off the set wiping sweat from the palms of their hands; the camera, intent on a Palladian façade, might have strayed only a few yards and found scaffolding and two-walled rooms. To him, who would have loved the human personality to be as static as a flower on a stalk, unmarred by emotions, unclogged by frustration, the most intimate and disordered side of people was displayed. The foibles, the strange quirks, odd growths, darknesses, contradictions which novelists care so much for, he found less delightful. Though loving people, he loved stillness more, and visual beauty. He desired the woman who would never raise her voice, nor snivel into a handkerchief, nor encroach on another's private territory. He did not marry. He collected pictures. He collected especially the pictures which would help him to forget the cracked façades, the tear-stained faces which dogged him always. Until he saw a picture Frances had painted.

It was before the war, on a late winter's afternoon toward tea-time: one of the days when Spring seems suddenly possible; nothing is different but the knowledge that it is not yet dark and yesterday would have been. The sky is translucent between the buildings, and the flowers on barrows and in shop-windows are not winter flowers any more, but hyacinths and tulips and mimosa. The scent of lilac was fanned towards him, as if to compensate for the dwarf at the kerbside and the newspaper-placards about Hitler and Austria.

As he turned into a side street it began to rain, and there was Frances's picture in the window of an art gallery. It was a girl sitting on a sofa. It might have been his sofa: it was shabby and sagged at one end where she sat with her feet tucked up close to her body; her mouth drooped, her face was pushed up crookedly against her hand as she stared out of the picture; she was caught in an off moment; she was a little dejected, a little dishevelled: yet the room and she in it were pink and golden. Through Frances's eyes he saw all her life lying behind her, she was made to seem perfectly in context as he had never been able to see people before, as no writer could have shown him; only this painting had made a pattern for him which was at last intelligible.

The rain had come scattering down over the shop-window as hard as grain. He went on looking at the picture through the silvery drops, then through streams of oily rain which began to run down the glass like gin.

There are great paintings which are for everybody, and then there are lesser pictures which will reflect light only here and there, rather capriciously, to individuals. Life itself shifts round a little and what we had thought all whiteness, or all darkness, flashes suddenly, from this new angle, with violet and green and vermilion. So that old picture of Liz sitting on the sofa, seen through the rain-washed window, turned life a little under his very eyes, put beauty over the people in the streets, the dwarf, and a woman with dyed hair standing in a doorway, and even over poor Mrs Betterton crying in his room last night because her husband had left her, had propped the usual note on the usual chimney-piece and gone for ever.

He went home very much excited, perhaps exalted even. His landlady putting the supper on the table was bathed in rose colour; the cat yawned, the green stain ran into the bath under the taps, and Mrs Betterton coming again with the day's instalment of woe—all was radiance; through Frances's eyes could be made static and beautiful and set in a pattern.

This new excitement struck right through his personality and infected his work. He was a camera-man in those days. The camera, he saw, might alight like a butterfly and by its very act of choosing, make beautiful and significant whatsoever object was selected.

Month by month, year after year, Frances grew very close to him, dearer than any wife. Others might have done for him what she did—Vuillard, who at once came to mind, or Bonnard—but she was the one of his choice and he cultivated her in his mind and cherished her name.

He became a director; and then millions of eyes began to see through his the faces beyond the rain-washed pane (a favourite symbol), the landlady, the stained bath, the dwarf, the cat, the cripple, and Mrs Betterton sniffing into her crumpled handkerchief.

In those wide-set, spiritual relationships there is a time when the temptation to meet in the flesh becomes irresistible, just as after years of silent contemplation, there is the need to write the first letter. It had been a one-sided relationship, for Frances was a poor letter-writer. She wrote as a maiden-lady and not often at that. Yet he felt somehow that his own long, revealing letters were not unwelcome. If they were, he still must write them, sitting in his room at night, crossing the distance, he thought, into her very mind.

The letters, the piece of lace from Italy, the box of dates from Iraq, the picture-postcard of the Parthenon, the pressed gentian; all the different conditions under which he had contrived to get news to her during the war when he was caught up in soldiering, a prisoner in Germany; all that had made up his part of the relationship suddenly seemed insufficient. At long last, he must see her and talk to her. He risked more than he had ever risked before and sat in the train this Sunday evening as if he were at the end perhaps of a very long friendship.

And there was the great dog she had described. It was all as she had said, except that only one woman awaited him and not two. He had walked very slowly up the platform behind all the other people, towards this woman, who sat very still, very straight, in the evening sunlight.

And now, pacing beside him across the cobbled square, she said: "You were foolish to come, I think. I love her myself, but she is not like that. She is . . ."

She hesitated, for she could think of no way of describing Frances, and there, out of the porch of the Griffin, Richard Elton came with a girl on his arm, a palely-clad girl, with silk net gloves and long swinging hair. They paused on the pavement. Which way should they go? They argued, laughing, and finally set off, smiling at one another. Sickened and rebuffed, Camilla forgot what she was saying about Frances, forgot Morland Beddoes, too, and walked beside him in a sudden pained silence as if she had bitten her tongue.

He walked humbly beside her, his raincoat over his arm, swinging his little case.

"It is here," she said, and then—because he was after all so different from what she had expected—added: "It is rather awful, I am afraid."

"No." He stood still on the pavement and looked up at the shuttered façade. "No. I had thought of it being like this."

"You shall see. How fusty it smells!"

In the hall a pen scratched, a clock ticked. They were coffined-in from the bright evening. The proprietor sat at the desk, writing, and the Siamese cat watched him; he guarded the wet ink from its fur with his hand, as it curved its paw out to catch the pen. He watched Mr Beddoes signing the book as if he had enticed him into doing it, smiling neatly. The cat suddenly narrowed its eyes, seeing Hotchkiss blundering about on the drugget, delighting only in what was at floor-level.

"I will show you your room." The old man came

slyly out of his little kiosk, as if it were a corner of a web, and led Mr Beddoes towards the stairs.

"In a minute we will have a drink," Mr Beddoes promised, looking up at the clock which still ticked away, but marked some impossible afternoon hour.

As soon as they had gone Camilla dragged Hotchkiss with her towards the desk and began to turn back the pages of the visitors'-book.

Suddenly, she saw the name; a child's hand, ornamented with little curls and weakly leaning first one way, then the other. Group-Captain Richard Elton. British. An address in London, S.W. She looked disdainfully at the page, and frowned; but her heart was thudding very fast.

Hearing voices, she snapped the book together, and put out her hand to the cat, taking its paw and smoothing it. Steadily, it beat its tail backwards and forwards, and dribble ran out of Hotchkiss's mouth as he watched.

"Good!" said Mr Beddoes, clapping his hands together, standing at the bottom of the stairs. "A drink," he suggested.

"It is a funny room up there," she said in a low voice. "I went to see it, but I could do no better."

"It was more than kind of you. And the view . . ."

"Yes, the view . . ."

The cat withdrew its paw from her fingers, as if it desired her whole attention, or none.

"Where could we drink?"

"I must warn you that . . . that Frances is expecting you . . . she will be tart with me if we are late.

There will also be dandelion wine and you will have to drink it."

She did think he looked a little dismayed, but guessed it was not on account of the home-made wine. Perhaps some picture of Frances was emerging from her conversation, and a picture he was unwilling to see.

She led him into the bar and sat down at a tiled table in a corner. He fetched some gin and sat opposite her and said: "Perhaps it would be better for me to wait until tomorrow."

"She expects you tonight. She has a reason, I believe. I think she wants to see you first, and show you the pictures later. She will delay it and then say it is dark. You see, there is perhaps nervousness on her side, too."

Although she thought him mistaken, this strange relationship touched her, and was a vindication of something she had always liked to believe. A strand of invisible web had flown out from the elderly woman, had brushed by chance upon this middle-aged man, had enmeshed them both, netting them together in a curious intimacy. In a world of misunderstandings, of lights struck and sputtering out unseen, of one word spoken and a different heard, of clumsiness, of disappointment, this relationship seemed to her a miraculous thing. Coincidence works sometimes for good, she realised, and the light may fall on a friendly face before it flickers out, the voice that calls out may be answered. 'Yes, it is very wonderful,' she decided, 'but chancy, too. So much depending, for instance, on

whether he turned that evening into the side street . . .'
—for he was trying to describe the picture of the girl on
the sofa.

"Liz. It was Liz," Camilla interrupted.

When he was talking, he slid forward to the edge of
the chair, sitting sideways, one hand inside his jacket,
patting, stroking the shirt over his chest, his eyes never
off her face.

"Frances was her governess when she was a child.
She is there now, with her baby. You'll see her."

He looked at her without speaking, and then suddenly sat back in his chair.

"You are right. It was a mistake to come."

"What difference does Liz make?"

Presently, he leaned forward again, pushing his glass
out of his way impatiently. "Think of a picture you
know very well, perhaps you have been familiar with it
for years. It is static, unchanging. The world lies
frozen inside the frame. As if a hand pulled a lever and
all the traffic stood still. The smile never fades, the tear
never falls, the girl never ties her ballet-shoe: Madame
Vuillard is just going to water her hyacinths, and in a
moment Renoir's man will lower his opera-glasses and
his face will change. That Bar at the Folies-Bergère!
Suppose the barmaid awoke from that frozen moment—
the moment which we are so accustomed to, which has
lasted so many years—took up the rose and smelt it,
lifted her hands from the marble and poured out a
glass of Bass! All the mirrors would splinter, the world
disintegrate, the moment fly away into thin air. And I

133

feel that . . . Liz, did you say? . . . I feel that Liz
will break all the glass for me in the same way."

"But it isn't a famous picture like Manet's."

"It is far, far more important to me."

"Which will be better—for her to be different, or the
same?"

He smiled, but didn't answer.

"You are too romantic about your pictures," she said.

"I went back the next day, and the next. And the
day after that, I sold my watch and borrowed from my
friends and bought it. Now it's worth six times what I
paid. It hangs over the fireplace and I stare at it for
hours. You have to *live* with pictures. Like taking a
wife." He smiled. "Casual visits don't amount to the
same thing."

"I remember that picture being painted. Our first
holiday with Frances after we left school in Switzerland. I had forgotten, but now I remember it again.
It must be strange being a painter and sending one's
children away for ever. I had never thought of that
before. I think we must go."

He stood up at once. "I am very nervous," he said,
looking down at her.

"It will be all right." She lifted her eyes to his and
smiled. "I will help you," she said.

•   •   •   •

Frances sat at her dressing-table. The evening
sunshine flowed over the crystal and silver, over the
two pink zinnias in a glass whose lovely matt petals

were alone still in the flashing, restless, quivering light.

Along the landing, the baby let out a little wail at intervals. Just as she thought he had fallen into a sound sleep he would give another cry.

Footsteps crunched along the gravelly road on the other side of the privet hedge, people coming from chapel or going towards the pub, or townsfolk on a country walk. It was a beautiful evening. The valley was swathed in ripening corn, gardens clotted with blossom. Gnats rose in a golden haze under the elm trees.

Frances stretched her hand out into a shaft of light. She was wearing her mother's engagement-ring of pearls and garnets. She had never before put it on, nor done more than take it from its box and let it lie in the palm of her hand under the light. Now she turned it nervously, changing it from one finger to another, then from her left hand to her right.

She had been trying for a long time to raise her arm enough to comb her hair. She tried again, but the pain gripped her as hard as ever. In a sudden panic, unlike her, she tiptoed to the banisters and leaned over, calling Liz, very softly, that she should not awaken the baby. When she heard her answer, she went back to her room and sat down and then, just as Liz reached the landing, she wrenched the ring off her hand and dropped it on to the dressing-table.

"What is it?" Liz looked round the door.

"Why are you crying?" Frances asked, and their eyes met in the mirror.

"I'm not."

"Come here, Elizabeth. I asked why are you crying?"

Liz put the back of her hand across her eyes and turned aside, her mouth stiffening. "Harry . . . he seems so . . ."

"He's teething."

"Well, I . . . Frances, dear . . . I don't care for anything as long as Harry's well. Nothing else matters . . . Arthur, or . . . or anything."

"Arthur is part of Harry."

"I suppose so. What did you want me for?"

"I wondered if you would mind tidying my hair for me?"

"Of course."

Without thinking, she took the comb and drew the pins out of the thin, silvery hair which was like spun silk over the pink scalp.

"Take it up and roll it under—so!" Frances made sketchy movements with her left hand.

"What is wrong?" Liz asked.

"My arm. Rheumatism."

"I didn't know. How long has it been?"

"Some time. Getting rather worse lately."

"It shouldn't, in this lovely weather."

"I'm an old woman."

"Oh, nonsense."

"The times I've done *your* hair! Ringlets for parties— but they always fell out. It was better smooth, but you wanted curls."

"There!"

"Yes, that's good. Thank you."

Liz went to the window, the comb still in her hand, and looked out listlessly at the passing people. Frances picked up the ring and held it out to her. "Give me your hand!" she said. "I will enjoy giving it to you now. When I'm dead I shan't be able to see you wearing it."

A little put out, incredulous and embarrassed, Liz took the ring.

"But, Frances!"

"Don't say anything. Yes, it looks nice. And, my dear, don't fret about Harry. Don't be like that about him all his life. Anguished. And everything staked on him."

Liz turned the ring on her finger. "The anxiety bangs about inside me like a great box. My stomach aches with it."

She put her cheek against Frances's and closed her eyes. Her throat hurt intolerably and she tried to breathe slowly, to steady herself.

"I'm sorry about your arm . . ." Then suddenly she straightened and drew away. "Your *right* arm?"

Frances nodded.

"You mean you can't paint?"

"Only for the time being. It will be all right," Frances said calmly, walking about the room, touching one thing after another, as if to steady herself. "It will get better. In any case, I'm old . . ." ('But I wouldn't have wished to stop here,' she thought. 'Not on *this* note. Not with those paintings.')

137

In the silence the gate banged and Liz, drying her eyes on the lace curtains, said: "Here they are! The train must have been very punctual. Why, he's . . ."

"He's what?" Frances said sharply, standing far back in the room.

"He's . . . well . . . rather fat and . . . They've disappeared now."

Camilla and Mr Beddoes had stepped out of sight into the flower-covered porch.

Frances was very white. She stood still by the empty grate.

Then: "Run and open the door," she snapped, and closed her eyes as if she were praying.

CHAPTER TEN

"EVERY WORD we said was wrong."

"I tried until my head ached, but the ice creaked all the time. It was so thin, I could see the weeds lying under it."

Camilla ran her hand through one of the stockings she had taken off, stretching it against the candlelight.

"Near the heel," Liz said, peering too. "You've kicked your ankles."

"Oh, damn."

"Mend it now while I feed Harry."

"I felt so dreadfully sorry for them both. And that whale-boned act of Frances's. Misery from beginning to end."

"She's ill, you know."

"And he had woven fantasies about her for so many years and never stopped himself to ask what he anticipated."

"It must be hard—to expect some sweet romantic understanding and to get only polite conversation."

"About the fruit crop . . ."

". . . and the habits of bees."

"I liked especially holidays in Bournemouth."

"No talk about paintings. Each time he began she tacked away from him and grew rather vague . . ."

"As if it wasn't quite nice . . ."

". . . in mixed company."

Liz smoothed back her baby's hair. It was very fine and clung to her fingers.

"Do you think he looks blue?"

Camilla glanced over her shoulder. She was sitting in the best of the candlelight, the stocking over her fist, darning.

"Harry, I mean," Liz said. She looked down at him lying on her lap. "He seems so *veined*."

"Oh, no, I don't think so." Running her hand out of the stocking, she examined her work carefully. "It's ruined anyhow."

"But don't you think his eyelids look dreadfully mauve?"

Camilla went to the mirror and tried to look at her own eyelids.

"I've got freckles on mine," she said, suddenly staring at herself, forgetting Harry. She could see only that moment outside the Griffin, the girl whose hair swung on her shoulders—she had put up a little silk-gloved hand to it, in an affected gesture. 'The differences between women!' she thought. 'The irre-concilement, between her sort and my sort. When she brushed her hair back, tilted her chin to him, there was a horrible calculation in her flattery, making all my movements seem artless and clumsy as a pony's. And if I behaved like that, tried to gratify his vanity by such gestures, such affectations, I should hear my own laughter inside me. And as well as that, I am ten years too old.'

"It seemed a pity to wake him," Liz said regretfully. "After such fitful sleep."

'And what do I want with him after all?' Camilla asked herself. She scooped a froth of cream out of a pot and slapped it over her face, covering it until only her tired eyes showed, rather discoloured against the white.

"It always makes me heave when I massage under my chin," Liz remarked. She pinned her baby up and kissed him. "Not that I do very often."

'Something against next term is what I want,' Camilla thought, staring at the eyes in the mirror. 'Something against the long winter, if only a memory. Not to have to re-enter the school with all its bleak cleanness, its smells of paint and polish, with everything in me the same as when I left it, nothing added or taken away, nothing to remember and nothing to look forward to.'

"It was terrible when Frances tried to be polite and talk about films to him," Liz continued. "And the last film she saw was when I was a child and she took me to *Ben Hur*!"

Camilla suddenly smiled at her own leprous face in the mirror. "I imagine it is all done with models, Mr Beddoes," she quoted.

"He was so nice about it."

"And all those questions about Greta Garbo—as if he were bound to know."

"What would have happened to the evening if we had not been there?"

"*We* asked a lot of questions too."

"It was that sort of conversation. It didn't go free-wheel."

"In spite of the dandelion wine."

"Rhubarb."

Liz stood up, and the anxiety settled in her eyes again. She took Harry back to his cot and Camilla patted the cream under her chin, retching a little, her eyes watering.

. . . .

Frances stood in the dark garden while Hotchkiss crashed among the creaking cabbage-leaves after some small scuttling thing, too quick for him. When he had plunged away through the gap in the hedge, there was silence. She imagined him going over the harsh stubble of the field, his belly grazed by hollow stalks, his nostrils teased by drifting scents of fur and flesh: but he was a great blundering Caliban, unused to the traffic of the night, the maze of crossed and crossing scents, evaded always by the quick and feat.

The moonlight was enough to read by, the air humid as the inside of a flower. Orion seemed to hang and swing out across the sky like a man on a trapeze and, lifting her head, she thought: 'One glance at the sky finishes religion for me. I know then that we and all the clutter we have made upon the face of the earth— our fantasies and our myths—count for nothing. The scum of little houses, the Parthenon itself, all of our frail properties, will fly like dust into the abyss. For all civilisations are like elaborate campings-out, a complicated picnic in the face of nature's discomforts. And upon this impermanence we set up our easels and paint our pictures. What goes on to the canvas is the ticking of our hearts, the pulse of our lives. Yet when we die, what will happen? Other men and women will paint over our work; or those manifestos of ours against the indifference of the world will lie, face down, among old books and ornaments in junk-shops, in attics. Even if they hang in a gallery, framed and catalogued, respected and remarked upon, soon brown gravy will cover them, cracks and whorls will appear, the once radiant light will pour upon the scene like a sepia fog, the transparent petal will be dipped in glue: so that soon, only a pale face, a pale hand, will show in the darkness, and that face, that hand cracked over like mosaic. In the end, my heart-beats, my life's work, will fade away along with the rest, the Parthenon will go down on its knees like an aged elephant, and the embalmed words of the great will count for no more than Liz and Camilla chattering up there in the lighted bedroom.'

The garden was so quiet that when an apple fell into the flower-border she started. Then the silence seemed more intense than ever. 'When the rottenness has begun in it, it drops,' she told herself. 'It is either better or worse with people. For here am I, an old woman, but still hanging on the tree. In both compassion and in cruelty we outstripped nature long ago.'

She whistled for Hotchkiss, but he did not come. Now the light went out in what she called 'the girls' room', but the talk went on, and the low gusts of laughter.

'No one ever came to me,' she thought. 'I never lay in bed and talked to anyone. But I felt tenderness for people, and love. Hid it, though, with my prim ways as soon Camilla will, and from the same motives, fear and pride. Pride does not come before a fall. Nothing happens after pride. It closes the way. Life does not come to us. Or comes too late. And if it does, comes because of someone-else's humility, a little miracle, a man like Mr Beddoes who was brave enough to set his own charity, his own warmth, against my exclusiveness, and did indeed try to break through the briers and pass the sleeping sentries—but forty years too late, alas, when I am at the point of death and sit alone, hedged round by convention, and my set ways, and shyness . . . and those two chattering girls who denied us our peace together, so that each time a silence fell, they flew into it with their nonsense like a couple of jays.

'It is very strange,' she thought, 'that the years teach us patience; that the shorter our time, the greater our capacity for waiting.'

So twisted round in her thoughts was she, that she did not hear Hotchkiss coming up the garden, or see his dark shape on the moonlit grass, was conscious of him only when he put his cold nose to her hand. She turned to go inside. 'And so,' she decided, shutting out the dark garden, bolting the door, 'not tonight, but another time, I may sit down with him and say all that I should like to say, but never have said except in my paintings. His humility must show me the way and teach me to wait, as he has waited.'

.   .   .   .

The moonlight was enough to read by and Morland Beddoes stopped to examine the gravestones in the churchyard, taking, he thought, a short cut towards the Griffin. The deep but narrowly incised letters, the dates all beginning with 17, the eighteenth-century names—Caroline, Sarah, Thomas, Anne—were all clear enough in this blanched light. "Great style," he said aloud, his finger-tips going from letter to letter across the stone as if the names were written in Braille. "Essentially English," he added. He bent and peered; he stepped on to the grass which so sparsely covered the cracked, parched earth. When he came to angels, to imported marble and black letters on granite from Aberdeen, he walked more quickly, and was conscious suddenly that his peerings and prowlings had not been unobserved, for loitering through the church from one tree to another, and laughing softly (perhaps, he thought a little self-consciously, at his strange behaviour) were a man and a woman, drifting together, entwined, and turning sometimes, between the infrequent lamps, to embrace one another more closely, their voices dropping to whispers, and from whispers to silence.

He hurried on into the street where the road ran like a great river, curving between the buildings and reflecting the repeated lights. Solitary always himself, he felt a great respect for lovers, as if, braver than he, they recklessly committed themselves to hazard.

Across the market square his footsteps rang metallically. Only here and there, on top storeys, windows blossomed into light.

One yellow light shone beyond the hall door of the hotel. 'Welcome' said the door-mat, but to those going out. The letter-rack was empty. A smell of gravy-soup and stale bread hung about, and at the bottom of the stairs, the little cat, its sides bulging, turned its paw delicately under its tiny tongue; then, seeing Morland, put its feet exactly together and shut its eyes, as if obliterating itself. He stooped to stroke it; incredibly silken it was, and its fur crackled to his touch.

'I don't have cats,' he thought, 'because they die, and that might hurt me. And I do not marry, lest my solitude should be invaded and my way of life violated. Not a very brave man, in fact.'

In from the street came Richard Elton. At the foot of the stairs they met.

'Yes, he is alight from that woman,' Morland thought, nodding a greeting, taking his hand from the cat and remembering how the other must have observed him reading the gravestones in the moonlight.

Both gave precedence to the other: at last Richard consented to go first. He ran up the staircase, going lightly like an athlete, his hands in his pockets, jingling loose coins, his trousers drawn tight across his buttocks, which, Morland decided, looked arrogant somehow, and then absurd. He disappeared among the dark passages off the first landing where the smell of gravy-soup became practically visible, as if mirrors, pictures and wallpapers were all dipped in it.

More slowly, breathing more heavily, Morland followed. It had been a momentous day for him and he was tired. Although his sense of relief was deep, it did not diminish his weariness.

He sent himself out on his adventures as if he were two people—perhaps a pearl-diver and another man who would await his return. Bringing back treasure to himself made life worth living, as it was tonight, and his years as a prisoner of war had made him miserly of this treasure which he turned over so privately; for then it was all he had that could not be violated. He spun out the hours with it, lying on his bunk on Sundays as rain hit the windows, or on a winter's evening as the others played cards or argued round the stove. He threw no stories into the common pool, shared no women with them in retrospect; tried to remember suitable stories but could not, and when he looked back on his life in England before the war was left with nothing to recount, had lived too mildly, chaperoned himself too closely; made little money, was never unseemly drunk, had got the better of no one; had slept, indeed, with two women but not, he must admit, at once. His love-making he saw now was too undistinguished to be acceptable to the others who, as the months, the years went by, recalled out of the void always more bizarre, more terrifying orgies. He was relieved that he had nothing he could share, and turned over his treasure quietly, trying to print on his closed eyelids the pictures he had seen, or faces he had loved. And the others left him alone, he was too good-tempered to bait; they respected him in a way, though putting upon him the most unpleasant of the work because of his education; but no offence was meant, none taken.

Sometimes Frances wrote to him, with enquiries after his health, hoping this, hoping that; with news that the study of a woman combing her hair was finished and that she was knitting him a pair of socks (which she was not allowed to send): a few remarks about the weather rounded off the rest. And it was good that she wrote thus, he felt. With painting and knitting in the same sentence.

He crossed the bedroom and drew back the curtains. The sky was like a swan's breast, flocky in the moon-light. He saw the cobbled square dramatically, as if soon a foreshortened figure would emerge from the shadows bent on some film-adventure. The church clock struck a quarter, and an express train raved incoherently through the station, blowing golden smoke to left and right.

'Yes, this evening,' he thought, leaning out into the lovely air, 'all this evening, everything was right: her shyness, her charity, her good behaviour. If I spoke of painting it reminded her of my wine-glass. And the old-fashioned room, the parlour she called it, the lace curtains, the plants in pots, the ticking clock, were all that I had imagined from those letters of hers I had in Germany; even her appearance, her voice, her turn of phrase; and her governessy hold on those two young women; it was all as if she were saying: "I am the maiden-lady life made of me, and the painter I was born to be, and the two things are the same." '

He drew the curtains and inspected the room, opening drawers and cupboards, took the ewer and stood it over a hole in the floor-boards to keep out mice or anything worse which might emerge in the night; then he began to undress.

The church clock struck another quarter and, overhead, footsteps went up and down at intervals, as if someone paced the room unable to sleep.

.   .   .   .

The bed was littered with newspapers. Richard had been lying down among them, staring at the ceiling, his arms crossed under his head. Now he was walking up and down smoking. He was unnerved tonight. Meeting that fat little man in the hall had upset him. He had seemed to be waiting for him, standing about at the bottom of the stairs stroking the cat, had loitered in the churchyard, pretending to read the gravestones, would not precede him up the stairs, but came slowly after, watching and observing.

Unlocking his suitcase he swept the papers into it on top of the dirty collars, rolled-up socks. He took out his diary and laid it on the dressing-table. Putting his hand in his pocket he brought out the head of a red rose-bud. It was warm and soft and he held it tightly in his hand, walking up and down the room, trying to still himself, irritated by the memory of the girl he had taken into the country, had kissed in the churchyard; bored, laid waste by the tedium of love-making. She had given him the rose, warm still from being pinned to her clothes, as if she expected him to find it enhanced from being there. He opened his hand and the scent escaped from the bruised petals, sweet and clovery.

He sat down, and unlocked his diary, like a man driven by habit and hopelessness, to a drink he has deferred. Turning the last few pages, he read 'Camilla' again and again, spelt first one way and then another. He put his head down on his arms across the opened book. He must get to her, he knew. In the morning he must find her and elude that man who waited for him on the stairs; malignant, sinister, calmly prepared to remain there for ever if need be; a little cloud which had arisen no bigger than a man's hand over this sunny little town.

He took up his pen and then, seeing that furled rose lying there, became disturbed again, and afraid. He picked it up and went to the window. All the square lay empty before him, the cobbles shining like soapsuds under the lamplight. He imagined the rose dropping downwards in a great arc, lying there until morning; incriminating; the little slip which leads men to their death in murder-stories, in films.

Frightened now, he moved back into the room with the rose crushed up in his hand.

. . . .

When the baby cried in the night no one heard. Only Hotchkiss got up from under the kitchen-table and lumbered to the door. He stood there with his head bowed listening for a second, and then settled down again, but with one eye opening from time to time.

CHAPTER ELEVEN

EVENING LIGHT came through the dusty windows. In the long pause between the soup and the steamed turbot, Camilla pleated the tablecloth above her lap, even took up the wine-list and began to fringe its edges, until Richard took it gently from her hands.

The fish had shrunk from its blueish bones, was covered with gluey skin, and accompanied by broken potatoes and a little pool of water.

"Even when we've eaten it, we shan't be done with it," Richard said, shifting it about on his plate. "The stench is with us for the evening."

"We could go out."

"Why are you so nervous?"

"I don't know."

She glanced about her, but Mr Beddoes did not appear. She dreaded a meeting between the two men. The dining-room was nearly empty. A young woman took bones out of her mouth on a fork with an air of worried refinement, darting only an anxious whisper at the man opposite; a waitress leant against a sideboard picking varnish off her nails.

"I looked for you all day," Richard said.

Anything more than a whisper was heard all round

the room. The waitress glanced across at them.

"But why? Why?" Camilla murmured.

"I dreamt about you last night."

"Hush!"

"I dreamt you were picking apples off a tree and handing them down to me. I felt so—very peaceful. And you smiled. Sometimes, things come clear in dreams, so that you are made to understand about people what you hadn't realised before; you never see them again in the same way. So this dream showed me that you make me feel steady and peaceful. I thought it meant that you would be coming to see me as you promised. All the morning the dream hung about me. I was afraid to leave the bar."

The waitress folded her arms across her chest and yawned and yawned until her eyes watered.

"It was so difficult for me."

"They say dreams don't have colours, but this one was so vividly green and red. The apples and the grass . . ." He could imagine deep orchard grass, polished apples brilliant between the leaves; the scene was as plain to him as if he had really dreamt it. Camilla saw it very plainly too. The waitress thought it nonsense. She came to take their plates. All they had done to the food was to rearrange it.

Camilla thought: 'We are like two people on the opposite sides of a river, and though we strain our voices they cannot carry from one bank to the other.'

The dreary food passed between them on the table. Even the stewed apple seemed to have bones in it. The girl at the other table took bits out of her mouth with her spoon.

"You see, I am in great trouble," he said, and drew four lines down the tablecloth with his fork.

She tried to skim cigarette-ash off the top of her coffee, but her hand shook.

"I need you to help me."

"Let us get out of here."

She put the spoon in her saucer and dropped the napkin on the table with a gesture of weariness and finality.

He followed her out of the dining-room.

Mr Beddoes saw them as he came down the stairs, watched Richard guiding her along the drugget, a hand under her elbow. They did not see him, and he went at once to the hotel register which lay on a ledge by the office and began to turn over its pages.

Richard and Camilla pushed their way along the street, past the queues at the bus-stops and the cinemas and outside the station. Soon they came to a little park full of paper-bags and bus tickets, where children were playing in the dust under the trees, and they sat down on a wooden seat, rather apart from one another.

When she turned to look at him, he was sitting a little sideways, staring at her, his arm resting along the back of the seat. He opened his hand and she put hers rather timidly into it. People went by on the asphalt paths, looking at the calceolarias, the lobelias, the beetroot-coloured leaves of the weird municipal flowers in the crescent-shaped beds.

"I saw you last night," she suddenly said, and at once his fingers were very still, twined in her own.

"Where?"

"Outside the Griffin."

He waited.

"With a girl," she added carelessly and then waited too.

His hand slipped up her bare arm but he said nothing.

Sparrows took dust-baths at their feet. They both watched them without seeing.

"If you were there, why didn't you come for me?" he asked.

"I'm most relieved that I didn't."

"You know I hate to be left alone."

She smiled primly.

"You should have saved me from that girl."

"Oh, women are always a temptation. 'Please, sir, it wasn't me, sir.' Yes, slaves or courtesans; destruction or inspiration." Her hand trembled on his arm. "Either a shadow between man and God or a devil in the bed."

"You certainly don't like men."

A woman sauntering by on her husband's arm turned her head curiously, as if she awaited Camilla's answer; but some instinct drew her back again to her child, who ran before her along the path; she called him sharply away from the flowers he would have liked to have picked, smiled as he put his fingers into the jaw of a great red bloom cowering under its own leaves. It was their evening walk, Camilla thought. They would comment on what they saw, but not talk to one another, for they had said long ago all that was to be said. The wife would look disapprovingly at those who sat hand in hand on the park seats, as if they threatened her world which she had built up straw after straw from one such moment of her own. They would return to this world in silence, locked-up from another; she would put the child to bed; he would turn on the wireless. Later, they would sit over a meal which was no longer the sacrament it once had been; he would yawn; she would stare in front of her. There they were for the rest of their time, separated from one another, but also, because of one another, separated from the world.

"The truth is that I know nothing about men," she said, looking after the woman, who had now caught up the small, wandering child and was holding him out behind a tree, her hair blowing over her flushed face, while her husband stood by smiling. "You don't understand what my life has been. No man would understand what life is like for so many women. How can we take any of the things we want, that you expect to have—freedom, adventure, experience—without being taxed intolerably, or making ourselves ridiculous in other people's eyes, or in our own?"

"Some women do take them."

"Most women don't."

"In the war . . ."

"But I'm talking about life, not death. Death

isn't an adventure, whatever Peter Pan may have hoped, but the end of adventure."

With the tips of his fingers, he traced a vein down the inside of her arm. "Were you never in love?"

"What my being in love amounted to would amuse you and amaze you."

She could remember herself as a young girl, never successful at those dances where she would hover at doorways, unclaimed; or comb her hair for ten minutes at a time in the deserted cloakroom. For no young men scribbled on her programme, only the avuncular whose wives led them to her, partly from kindness, but partly, she even then suspected, to keep them from the bar. She had despised her own over-animation with these middle-aged men, as if she must stun them into remaining; and then, as the years went by, the cold distaste she displayed instead, the sarcasm.

"Tell me!" Richard insisted, busily smoothing the fine gold hairs on her arm, ruffling and smoothing them.

"It would have been ignominious, but nobody saw . . . before that I hadn't shared anything secret, not even a glance, with another person. The feeling was new to me and very exciting."

"What did he look like?"

"Thin, dark, so white-skinned that he didn't tan in the summer like other people, but turned a kind of mauve." She laughed, and then suddenly frowned and turned his hand palm upwards. "What a terrible scar! How did you do that?" It ran across his hand, thick and crimson.

His face became closed and stubborn. "*I* didn't do it."

She stared at him beseechingly, but he gave her no comfort.

"I don't care to talk about it." He handed her a cigarette. "Go on telling me about that man."

But how could she? The nineteen-forties impinged on the nineteen-twenties; such darkness lay over the nostalgia that it seemed not sweet but meaningless. Ugliness has the extra power of making beauty seem unreal, a service beauty seems rarely able to return.

"What happened?" he was asking.

She struggled to go back. "At a party . . . one of those big Cambridge houses, and during one of those hiding games young people play. I went into a room on my own. It was cold and quite dark. I stood there shivering in my thin frock, and suddenly a hand went over my mouth and drew me back behind a curtain."

She could remember the plush smell of the curtains now, and the harshness of them against her bare arms. Enfolded by them, they stood close and whispering, his lips stroked her cheek, he closed her eyelids with his kiss. The moonlight came in through the window over the floorboards of the strange room, and down below footsteps ran along passages, doors banged, and all at once laughter rang out, for the game was over.

"I was only eighteen," she said, as if to excuse herself.

"What happened?"

"They came to find us. When I went down, the

lights frightened me. There was a great brilliant table, rocking with jellies and blancmanges. I couldn't eat. I felt that what had happened was stamped all over me, that they must all know. I kept touching my hair, smoothing my dress. Once he looked at me, and for a moment it was as if we were alone again, in silence. The next day he went back home. I cried, with the utter dreariness and desolation of life without the hope of seeing him, languishing in the attic, my only safe place, snow blowing past the windows."

"Didn't you see him again?"

"Yes. The next year he came again. There was a dance and I knew that he would be there. I felt ill with nerves. A year had passed, but I wasn't really a year older, for nothing had happened to me but day-dreams. As soon as I went into the room I saw him. I thought that my legs would fold up if I tried to dance with him. But I needn't have worried, because he didn't ask me. I don't think he remembered me. And I had dreamed of him for a whole year; he was always at the back of my thoughts and in bed at night there were all the scenes I went over and over, the things we should say to one another, our future together . . ."

"Don't laugh at it," he said quietly. He turned her hand and put a little kiss into it, moved by her innocence.

"I once told Liz all this, but rather jokingly."

"We suffer most when we are young," he said sententiously.

"I started off on the wrong foot and nothing went

right after that. I felt rebuffed for years, and never loved anyone, but Liz. I know it was a fault in me. I know I ought to have recovered from something which is after all only a part of growing-up. Liz would have. She always gives herself a second chance."

"That isn't always possible."

"Why did you say that you were in trouble?"

"Did I say that?"

"Why of course. Back in the hotel."

"It isn't really true; or when I am with you it stops being true. I mean, I don't think of it."

"I wish you would tell me."

"Then I will. I am in trouble about money." He laughed.

"What sort of trouble?"

"The usual sort. I haven't any."

"Are you in debt?"

"That *is* what happens to people who have no money."

"What are you going to do?"

"I think it will soon be time to make a move."

She looked so dreadfully shocked and anxious that he laughed again; but his eyes never smiled.

"Don't worry. I like contriving. It gives me something to do."

"A job would give you that," she said awkwardly.

"Would it, my sweet?"

He hid his displeasure with teasing.

"You can't go on for ever leaving a trail of debts behind you wherever you go."

"Can't I? Perhaps in your school-teachers' world I couldn't."

"But . . ."

"Have a cigarette."

"But . . ."

"Listen, sweetheart. I loved your girlhood's memories; they touched me and charmed me. But my life never was like that."

"I see now that it must have sounded pathetic beyond words to you. I thought so half-way through, but you made me go on."

"Not at all. I enjoyed it."

"Your acquaintance with brutality has brutalised you."

He glanced at the scar on his hand, then closed his fingers over it.

"In the end, *they* won, however brave you were at the time," she said. "They managed to implant the germ of their cruelty in you. As children who are bullied at school take it out of the still younger ones. You have let them cancel out your courage."

"You look better when you are angry."

"And this book you say you are writing—you will go on writing it, or not writing it, for the rest of your life. It will be your excuse, your refuge. Even the worst sort of book requires diligence. Requires a certain amount of time spent *out* of bars, *out* of the society of women."

She saw the picture of the girl with him outside the Griffin, how they laughed together.

"Of course, I know all this is simply green-eyed jealousy," he said.

To the passers-by, they were in the midst of a lovers' quarrel, a little tiff preceding a sweet reconciliation at nightfall.

'I should get up and walk away,' she told herself. 'I should go back to Liz and Frances and behave myself in future.' But she sat very still instead and watched the sparrows, traced a pattern in the dust and the blown sycamore seeds, with her sandal.

"Darling, let's walk through the gardens and pretend that we are married like all these other people!" he said, and he put out his hand and drew her up and tucked her arm into his. She walked with him along the asphalt paths, as if she were in a dream, sedate and bourgeois, like a painting by the Douanier Rousseau. Mr Beddoes would appreciate it, she thought; this domesticity among the savage leaves; the family-groups against the arid landscape.

A broken fountain dropped water unevenly over lily-leaves and floating bus-tickets, beneath which goldfish seemed suspended; pouting, debauched-looking fish with trailing veils. Pausing to look at this littered water, they both began to speak at once, she with a belated reprimand, he with an apology. The words rushed together and broke off at the impact.

They resumed their walk.

"What have you been living on since you came out of the Air Force?" she persisted.

When he did not answer her she glanced up at his

face and was struck, as she always was being struck, by his lack of expression, a curious emptiness, as if the broader emotions were the limits of what he could convey—laughter, fury, or self-pity.

"Air Force," he said lightly, like an echo.

"You don't listen to me."

He gathered himself together and squeezed her arm against his side. "Yes, I listen, sweetest. You asked what I live on. My gratuity, which now has come to an end."

"It must have been quite a lot," she suggested.

"Oh, naturally, hell of a lot."

"How much?"

"Never you mind. You ask too many questions, my lovely one."

'These endearments wouldn't matter to most women,' she mourned to herself. 'They wouldn't even hear them.'

"What are you going to do then?"

"I told you."

"And how long will you do it for?"

"Another three weeks. Then, whether I've got ahead with my book or not, I'm going into a friend's business. You look so relieved. You believe in the virtue of work, in everyone being boxed up and having pay-packets."

"I believe that in three weeks' time, you'll be in prison, not in business."

"Well, it can't be helped. There's no place for me until then."

"Couldn't you borrow money to tide you over?"

"There is no one to lend it. I wouldn't ask my father, and my mother's dead. All my friends are like me, or still racketing through the last of their gratuity, trying to turn the saloon-bar into the officers' mess."

"Well, then, I would lend it to you," she said stiffly.

"I don't borrow money from women."

"I think that's what my brothers would have called a personal code. Once in a pub I heard a man say: 'I don't have women call my beer for me.'"

"Neither do I."

"People who have personal codes do such dreadful things."

"Why did you offer to lend me money?"

"I thought it would be better for you than going to prison, but it doesn't matter."

"Would you do the same for anyone?"

"Some people I should be glad to see in prison."

"Not me, though?"

"You deserve better. You are still suffering from the war, and you need to recuperate, I suppose. You wouldn't do anything really bad." She smiled hopefully.

Suddenly a little child ran blindly against her, pursued by other children in a game. She steadied him, and when he cried at the shock, she tilted his face up and wiped his eyes.

"Would you marry me?" Richard asked, above the child's head.

.   .   .   .

Liz went quickly along the lane, her sandals slapping softly on the tarry road. All the evening Fair caravans had been passing the cottage and now, as it grew dusk, the last of them were slowly overtaking her. Children sitting on the steps looked at her incuriously; the short sturdy fathers stared ahead.

At the Green, the dusk was falling over a spangle of lights as the little temporary world was set up. But she could not pause to watch. Shut into the evil-smelling telephone kiosk, she spread out the coins which were hot from her clenched hand and took up the receiver. She thought it best to rehearse nothing, to let anxiety rush along the lines towards Arthur; it would relieve her to be incoherent, as she was bound to be.

She could imagine him sitting at his desk. He would swivel round in his chair, reach for the telephone, his voice at first casual, non-committal, as if he were hardly there and certainly could not be at everybody's beck and call.

She had waited until this hour for two reasons: the first, that her anxiety had grown worse as darkness began to fall; the second, that she knew what his evenings were—the recalcitrant curate called in to listen to a talk beginning: "To be perfectly frank . . ." and ending: "However, I appreciate your sincerity." Then young people perhaps coming in about their weddings, the conversation about banns and prices, mixed up with meaningless (to Liz) phrases, full of Latin words such as "cohabit" and "extra-marital relations". The poor young people. He would briskly tie up their vague feelings about one another into separate packets, label and pigeon-hole them. They would leave looking bewildered, inadequate, sullen, and would, Liz always thought, smiling at them in the hall on their way out, quarrel before they could reach home.

The telephone seemed to ring and ring in the empty house, that house upon which Liz made no mark but untidiness, since it was all complete when she arrived, settled into a rhythm which she could never change. Mrs Taylor—that wretched woman: bleak, inexorable, casting sadness about her—established there as house-keeper years before with her unalterable time-table. On the first Monday in March the sweep arrived (unrequested, since he too was accustomed to the Vicarage rhythm); loose-covers were changed seasonally; linen day was Tuesday; silver day Friday; pudding followed pudding in ordered sequence; fish-days came round as they should. And over it all fell Mrs Taylor's sighs, her bad heads, her preoccupation with suicide— "Why I don't put my head in the gas-oven and be done with it, I don't know"—for her life had been sad, catarrhal, colourless, her hair prematurely grey and her love for her husband only discovered alas after he had died. Although he now returned to her at night (against the vicar's orders, for Arthur objected to Spiritualism), his remarks, like those of most spirits, were banal and earthbound in the extreme. So disappointment dogged her and was there now in her cautious voice at the other end of the line. She was a little breathless, too, for she had been in the garden picking loganberries—"such as the birds had not already disposed of, or the maggots eaten away".

"I'm sorry to have brought you indoors, Mrs Taylor."

"That's quite all right. It's been constant all the evening, the telephone-bell . . ."

"Anyone for me?"

"No, all for the vicar."

"Did he say what time he'd be back?"

"Not too late, he said."

"Oh, I see."

"Shall I give a message?"

"No." She felt dulled and defeated; anxiety clogged her still. "No, it doesn't matter. Tell him I'll telephone again tomorrow."

"Don't forget the conference at Oxford."

"Oh, no. No."

"How is baby?"

"He's teething."

"They're a nuisance to us from the time we get them till the time we lose them, teeth."

"That's true."

"Well, there's another ring at the door, if you'll excuse me . . ."

"Of course. Goodnight, Mrs Taylor."

"Goodnight, madam."

Even after the little click she still held the receiver to her ear, as if she might perhaps be able to discern faintly the voices at the front door: then she carefully replaced it and tried to gather herself to go home, tried to draw herself out of that hall, from the voices she would have liked to have heard, the cards on the hall-table she would have liked to have spread out on the tray. She wondered where Arthur had gone, who had telephoned him all the evening. But firmly, Mrs Taylor shut her away from her own home, with her dull voice, her negative manner.

'Oh for a Mrs Parsons!' she thought, wrenching open the swing door and taking a good breath. 'Oh for someone warm and gossipy! The cups of tea we could dawdle over at the kitchen table; and the talk of disease and funerals, which seems so often to indicate a great zest for life!'

Now it was much darker; light shone behind the lace curtains of the caravans, and the dusk was like a sediment sinking down through the sky.

The Fair children, with their skimming and darting movements, their thin cries, were like gnats, Liz thought, standing for a moment to watch. A girl with silver bracelets up her dirty arms hung out a tea-cloth for the night air to bleach.

Tomorrow, the great roundabout would go up. Liz knew it well, the names of the horses off by heart. It was part of her holidays.

"One day Harry . . ." her thoughts began, as she turned back up the lane and then her pace suddenly quickened. She was almost running along between the hedges, as if she were afraid.

. . . . .

"You see," said Mr Beddoes, going down the path with Frances, "I hate those great agonised pictures, which say 'I', 'I', all the time. 'I am crucified.' 'I suffer.'"

Frances walked even more slowly. She picked a sprig of mignonette and twirled it in her fingers, sauntering and delaying, like a child going up to bed.

"That little picture of yours," he was saying, "the lemons lying on some spotted laurel leaves in a dish, it is so simply, so honourably done. As if you sat down for a long time and looked at the dish and thought about what it was and didn't begin to paint until you knew, better than anybody else: and, although you never said 'I', *because* you never said 'I', you shine through it like the sun."

They were at the door of the shed, which gave off a smell of creosote in the still warmth of the late evening.

"How can I see in this light?" he asked, standing by her as she unlocked the door. With the key in her hand, she stood for a second on the threshold.

"You will hate these paintings," she said. "But you must remember that people change—even at *my* time of life a woman can change. I committed a grave sin against the suffering of the world by ignoring it, by tempting others with charm and nostalgia until they ignored it too."

"By looking at one thing, we must always ignore another."

"How stuffy it is in here!" She was busy lighting a lamp. As the blue coronet of flame reached upwards, her hands guarding it looked transparent.

"I always felt," she said, "that life's not worth living; that I could only contemplate little bits of it and keep my sanity; and those bits I selected carefully—the sun on a breakfast-table, girls dressing, flowers . . ."

"But it wasn't all happy. Sadness often looked out of those girls' eyes . . ."

"An English sadness. Delicious to contemplate."

"The picture of Liz on the sofa—she was a woman alone in a room; as only God, I should have thought, could ever possibly have seen her. It was the truth."

"All *little* things," she said impatiently, blowing out a match.

"But *not* little. That *is* life. It's loving-kindness and simplicity, and it lay there all the time in your pictures, implicit in every petal and every jug you ever painted."

"Life's not simplicity," she said slowly. "Not loving-kindness either. It's darkness, and the terrible things we do to one another, and to ourselves. The sooner we are out of it the better. And paintings don't matter. They are like making daisy-chains in the shadow of a volcano. Pathetic and childish."

She sat down on a kitchen-chair and looked at the lamp burning; her clenched hand beat nervously against her thigh.

"The only thing that makes sense of it all is looking up at the sky at night and knowing that even the burden of cruelty we've laid upon the earth, scarcely exists: must fly away into dust, is nothing, too infinitesimal to matter. All the time, the house is falling into ruin, and I run to the walls and tack my pretty pictures to them as they collapse."

He went over to her and took her hand.

"You don't want me to see these paintings."

"They reject all that you cared for. I don't want you to feel too—dismissed."

"Who else has seen them?"

"Only Elizabeth."

"And what did *she* think?"

"What did she think? I didn't ask her. She's only a girl."

He smiled.

"What are you going to paint next?"

"I've finished."

"Why this blank canvas then?"

"If my rheumatism ever gets better, I may paint one more."

"Then it will have to be a summing-up. Which side will you come down on? Violence, or charity?"

She looked out of the window. After a moment she said: "Perhaps you are the devil come to tempt me."

"Whatever you put on this canvas, I claim. Because I love you. Whatever you choose to say, I shall hold dear. I have always cherished you and promoted you, and now I only want you to be yourself. I want you to be quiet inside and listen to yourself, as patiently as you once looked at those lemons and those leaves."

"Yes, I think you really are the devil."

"This is the first moment we have been alone."

"The girls are always here in August."

"You are three unhappy women under one roof."

"Unhappy?"

"Liz is unhappy about her baby. Camilla—that's a lovely name. It has the smoothness of ice—she's unhappy about her life; embittered, waspish. You're unhappy about the world."

"You have soon summed us up. The baby is only a passing anxiety. Elizabeth is never miserable for long. She's just a young and inexperienced mother feeling fussed. Camilla's at a forked road. She believes that what she doesn't take now, she'll never have. But will dwindle into an old maid. I am a terrible example to her. Her job shows her others."

He wondered if he should tell her that he had seen Camilla in the Griffin that evening, and decided he should not.

"What is she going to do?" he asked instead.

"She is never frank with me."

"Perhaps you frighten her."

"I think in that mood she would do anything that cropped up," Frances said vaguely.

"Has she friends in the town?"

"None that I know of. It is a poor holiday for her; she and Liz seem estranged. But I cannot worry about them now. They are grown women."

He smiled. "They have suddenly shot up, as they say. It is very peaceful here. And a nice smell of turpentine and creosote, and size; and, I think, honeysuckle."

"Night-flowering stocks."

"Don't worry, will you? Not any more."

"I don't worry. I only wanted to confess my weakness before I died, as religious people do. I think I heard Elizabeth come back."

"Shall we never be alone like this again? Must we waste any more hours talking about Greta Garbo in front of the girls, as you call them?"

She stood up. "Elizabeth will wonder where we are."

She took the blank canvas down from the easel and put in its place another picture. As he came towards it, she stood back a little, holding the lamp in her left hand. He took from a case in his pocket a pair of steel-rimmed Army spectacles. When he had put them on, he went over and stood beside her, and in the wavering light confronted the white bones of the earth and dark figures scurrying against a violet sky.

.   .   .   .

Richard took a piece of the hotel writing-paper up to his room. He sat down at the marble washstand, and very carefully tore off the address from the top of the sheet. Then, in his childish, curly hand, he began his letter.

'DEAR MOTHER,
'Just to let you know I am O.K. I hope you and Dad are keeping fit and well.' He paused for a long time, bit his nails, altered the full-stop into a comma and added 'in this lovely weather.' Once that was done,

he felt defeated, for there was nothing more to write, but his request for money. No words led up to this. It would leap abruptly from the page however he wrote it. He enquired a little about his mother's sciatica, his father's allotment, and at last began on his own situation. He imagined them reading the letter; saw, without having to recall it, the little sitting-room, jazzy and orange, the pride of the nineteen-twenties, with its vase of cape-gooseberries, and his own photograph on the piano, an arm out of focus to display his flight-sergeant's crown, rivers of light running over his brilliantined hair.

He thought of the unbearable evenings he had spent there on leave, his mother always anxiously watching him, ready to interpret the lightest sigh as censure, full of suggestions for passing his time, yet at once aggrieved if he fell in with any of them.

Now he had to think of the next stage of his travels, some address where money might be sent; but this, which should have been so easy, was most difficult of all. The frightening thing was that he was free to go anywhere and could not choose. Penzance, he thought. But why Penzance? Why not Bath or Edinburgh instead? So it went on. For nothing tied him. If people, employment did not, then surely sentiment would, his own memories, something even so faint as the reason why he had chosen this little market-town— once having, as a boy, camped with the O.T.C. up on the downs beyond the earthworks.

'Scarborough', he suddenly wrote. 'The Grand

Hotel, Scarborough.' He saw the empty wind-swept asphalt where he had drilled in front of that hotel in wartime, remembered the pettish gulls, the sea crashing on the beach below, the deserted water-front, whorled and entangled with barbed wire, the pale houses, the trees scrambling inland.

He did not imagine the streets crowded, hotels full, children with buckets and spades, a band playing, different barmaids. In his mind it was all just as he had left it. The decision had excited him. 'In three or four days,' he promised himself. 'They will send the money by return.' He sealed the envelope and put it into his pocket, and a great load was off his mind, he thought.

CHAPTER TWELVE

Liz slept badly, drifting in and out of thin, sleavy dreams, lying awake for timeless stretches. Once she thought Camilla was awake too and she said her name softly but there was no answer. 'But people don't go to sleep with their hands clasped under their heads,' she decided, and wished that she had not spoken.

After daybreak, the birds woke her. They burst in and out of the ivy, sang in the branches of the pear tree. A wash of new light lay over the ceiling. Harry stirred and whimpered in his little room and then cried aloud. Liz went softly across the landing and twisted him up in a shawl and took him back to her own bed. She lay on her side and looked at him and he wound his fingers in her hair, tried to catch her eyelids, her smile, all that moved on her face.

'Suppose there is a war!' she thought. 'Suppose that I bring him up to be civilised and sensitive and unsuspicious, and all that changes . . .'

"What's wrong?" Camilla asked suddenly, sitting up in bed.

"Harry cried, and I thought he might disturb Frances."

"Why are *you* crying?"

"Crying?"

"Well, of course you are."

"I didn't know." She brushed tears off her cheeks with her fingers. "I was only thinking about the war."

"What war?"

"If there is one."

"Well, what if there is?"

"It would finish our sort of civilisation for ever and ever."

"People said that last time. Anyhow, I think it is rather interesting to know something different might begin—perhaps tree-dwellers, or we might go down on all fours again and have another shot at standing up in a few thousand years' time."

"You wouldn't talk like that if you had a child."

"But Liz dear, don't begin the day with all this."

"I had such dreams all night. I wish something nice would happen. No one in my life goes in for treats. Arthur never does. Mrs Parsons told me that every dinner-time on washing-day her husband comes in and says: 'What about the pictures tonight, old girl?' to cheer her up. It must make her feel so nice—the kitchen all steamy, a smell of bubble-and-squeak, and something to look forward to in the evening, escaping into a different world—people in full evening dress, *suffering*. Very enjoyable to watch, I find it."

"Well, if all you want is to go to the cinema . . ."

"Mrs Parsons has such a happy life—all those outings she goes on with the Darts Team, crates of stout, lots of laughter, rude stories . . ."

"You don't like rude stories."

"I should do if I were Mrs Parsons."

"You would be worried about Euniss. Perhaps Mrs Parsons wishes she were safe and secure in the Vicarage."

"When you were out last night, I tried to telephone Arthur, but he wasn't there."

"He can't sit at home for ever lest you should happen to telephone."

"No, I know. But I so needed to talk to him. Frances and Mr Beddoes were discussing Greta Garbo again. I thought they would never stop."

"He's a good man."

"I think so. He's so good you forget he's there."

"I don't forget it. I find myself hoping that he thinks well of me."

"Harry looks better this morning."

"Liz, last night Richard asked me to marry him."

After an appalled silence, Liz said: "But you won't, will you?"

"I didn't say that to *you* when . . ."

"But Arthur's different. He's . . . well we both know what he is, but he isn't bad."

"Bad?"

"I'm sorry, but I think that Richard man is bad. I think he does harm. I'm afraid he will do harm to you."

"I'm afraid Arthur will do harm to you, too."

"Oh, no."

"He won't let you grow, or change. He will never

178

allow you to throw out new shoots, but will contort you into something he wishes you to be, a sort of child-wife. It's a kind of murder."

"Oh, don't exaggerate. You've always disliked him. And you're unjust to him."

"I love *you* so much. I want you to be happy."

('Is it true?' she wondered. 'Am I damnably possessive; worse than Arthur? The first time I wrote Liz's changed name on an envelope, I really suffered. A little thing, but I shied at the thought of it for weeks.')

"What did you say to him?" Liz asked.

"Oh, I said no."

"I don't understand it. What can you want with one another?"

"He wants security from me, I want adventure from him. Two opposite things. The dullness of my life attracts him, seems a refuge from all the adventure he has been through, the tension he suffers."

"Are you happy, then, when you're with him?"

"No, we are antagonistic to one another. But I suspect men and women always are."

"I hate that. If it's true. This child's bottom is really terribly chafed. I've done everything I can think of."

"Frances says he's teething."

"How can she know? I wish Mrs Parsons came to-day. She could tell me. I think it's too early to be cutting teeth."

"I daresay Euniss was born with hers. She has always seemed rather advanced for her age."

"And Arthur's at a Conference in Oxford. I just can't *get* him. Unless I write."

"What could Arthur do?"

"You don't understand."

"Is Morland Beddoes coming today?"

"He is sure to," Liz said indifferently. "Oh, the Fair is here. It came in last night."

"Well, there's your nice treat you were looking for. Mr Beddoes shall take you to the Fair."

"Of course, I shouldn't go," Liz said.

. . . . .

Liz sat on a golden horse, which was scrolled and gilded like all the rest, with outstretched legs and flowing tail, its buttocks painted with acanthus leaves. Each time she came round to them, she smiled. Arthur and Camilla standing stiffly by, smiled too; but primly, as if at a child. They could not speak to one another above the infernal forced-out music, and were tired of acknowledging Liz, and staring at the pivot of mirrors and panels of roses, a scene of chariot-racing and, unaccountably, polar-bears.

Mrs Parsons sat firm beside her husband, a trim little man wearing white plimsolls. She grasped the twisted brass rod with both hands and looked ahead, her American-cloth bag hanging from her arm.

Above the roundabout, the darkening sky was florid. All round, the dry feathery grass was strewn with litter. Every pole, each wheel and ladder or piece of wood, was painted with a coloured pattern; all the little misspelt notices were decorated.

Camilla and Arthur smiled hopelessly at one another, shuddered affectedly at the music. The noise roared in their ears. Liz, with her whipped-back hair, her bare feet in sandals, recurred now without their noticing. After a while, the horses slowed, so that the names painted below their manes could now be read—Flance, Eirene, Luna, Gilda, Florence. Arthur went forward and handed Liz down.

"I am so happy," she said. "It is so nice to see you in ordinary clothes."

Yes, he looked handsome in his flannels and his striped blazer which Liz called ordinary, Camilla thought, rather as if he would come down to the footlights at any moment and begin to sing. It was a pity for him that his job deprived him of the joy of wearing his school tie. But He had an oar on the wall of his study, Liz had told her, and silver cups which Mrs Taylor kept brilliantly polished.

Now Mrs Parsons was up in a swing-boat, one hand to her bosom as if it might fly away; she screamed like a peacock as she went higher. Liz watched her, but Arthur drew her away.

A girl with silver bracelets and rows of wooden rings up her dirty arms, shouting shrilly and mechanically, threw out the hoops to them, dropping their coins into her apron pockets. Ear-rings swung in her untidy hair, her face was tired, drained of vitality. Liz, trying painstakingly to encircle the undesirable objects, glanced at her with curiosity, wondered about her battered-down beauty. Each time she threw, her tongue came out between her teeth. Camilla cast her rings away casually. Arthur won a packet of soup-powder.

Mr Beddoes stood in front of a stall, eating a piece of yellow Swiss-roll. This annoyed Arthur, to whom it was enough of a concession to come to a fair without being seen eating its food.

He was easy in his mind now about Mr Beddoes, about whom he had felt a little curiosity, knowing nothing about film-directors, but wondering if the word did not indicate too much authority; a large man was suggested, with perhaps a megaphone, a man afraid of no one, calling actresses 'silly bitches', and expecting to be listened to, but not answered back. He disliked other men to have authority. He disliked other men. So he concluded that Morland was a tin-pot director of twopenny-halfpenny films, and indeed had never heard of any of the titles he had given in response to Arthur's own polite questioning. The stringy ties, the diffident voice and now the piece of Swiss-roll finished Mr Beddoes off completely.

"He is such a good man," Camilla was saying and she nodded at Liz and Morland sauntering on ahead.

"Oh, a very good fellow," Arthur said encouragingly.

"I don't just mean a good fellow. I mean 'good' as I imagine religious people mean it if they stop to consider."

"All right. Touché. And in what way does he show this?"

"I don't know. Perhaps by thinking ahead for

people. That's a rare kindness. It isn't even easy always to do the helpful thing at the right time, but he anticipates it and is ready. I've watched him with Frances."

"He's considerate and thoughtful," he suggested.

"Yes, but imaginative too."

"Imagination is a gift. We can't all have that," he said, as if she had reproved him for lacking it.

"I wonder!"

He put a penny in a machine and drew a card out of a slot. "Your fortune," he said, handing it to her as they walked on.

"You think imagination can be cultivated?" he asked.

"More than any other quality perhaps."

"And you value it highly?"

"Yes. Yes, I value it very highly," she said, tearing the card he had given her and dropping it to the ground.

"What was your fortune?" he asked.

"I don't choose to tell you."

He glanced at the torn pieces and then smiled at her. "I will imagine it instead."

"Well, do!"

"I shouldn't be sure that imagination doesn't often cause mischief."

"I believe that it's the people who are locked up in their own bodies who do harm."

Now Mr Beddoes had bought Liz a toffee-apple, and Arthur could not listen to Camilla any more.

"Of such is the kingdom of heaven," she said lightly,

following his glance. She felt stimulated by her conversation with him: he was enlivened, too. Their antagonism gave them freedom and impulsiveness. They fenced with skill and pleasure.

"She will be ill eating that," he said. "I shudder to think how or where it was made." He shuddered. Indeed, Liz now seemed to wonder the same thing and she dropped the apple behind a caravan. Mr Beddoes was laughing at her.

"Were you really worried about that?" Camilla enquired.

At first, she thought he wouldn't answer, then he said: "You detest me and suspect the worst of me. A bad thing to do, because so often people become what they are reckoned to be. You put words into my mouth that I have never said, and thoughts into my head that I could never think."

"Go on being gallant. Don't be pathetic," she laughed. "I have never hidden the fact that I detest you; so why accuse me of it as if I should deny it?"

"Ah, it is a bracing air we breathe!"

"Don't be affected."

"Why do you detest me? Why single me out?"

"Because you singled Liz out. Otherwise I should ignore you. Naturally her husband is important to me. She is dearer to me than anyone in the world."

He smiled the mysterious smile which meant that his adversary had betrayed herself in a way he need not underline in words.

Camilla walked unconcernedly on.

"My comment can scarcely be put into English," he said.

"Say it in Greek then," she said slyly.

"Ah, you are very quick."

"You don't believe it for a second, but you like to feel competitive."

Liz and Morland had paused, were looking back, waiting for them. It was getting late. The sky was quite dark, but for its red bruise above the Fair. Women were sweeping the slippery grass with besom brooms. Dirty, ringed hands counted money under the lamplight.

Arthur noticed the anxious glance that Liz gave Camilla.

"She can look after herself," he said, misinterpreting the look.

"We should go home. Frances will be waiting up for us," Camilla said.

"She's been painting all day. She'll be banging at the piano now," Liz said, and she hung back so that she could walk at Camilla's side.

Arthur went on ahead with Morland. The contrast between the two was amusing.

"Arthur is so *fine!*" Camilla laughed. "He should wear a laurel wreath. Let us make him one when we get back!"

"Yet it is Morland who is sure of himself."

"I like him. Why do you keep glancing at me in that anxious way? Do you think I have been flirting with your husband?"

Liz laughed. "No, as a matter of fact I don't think that."

"Would you mind if I did?"

"I should mind it dreadfully. Lady Davidson wouldn't be in it."

"I only asked as a matter of interest."

"Have you had a nice evening?"

"Yes, have you?"

"It was lovely to see Arthur, although there wasn't really any need."

"Any need?"

"As soon as I saw Harry's new tooth, I stopped worrying. A lovely tooth, as white as china. But it was kind of Arthur to come so far just for one evening. And kind of Mrs Taylor to tell him."

"Everything's kind and nice."

"Did you see Euniss Parsons this evening?"

"I saw Ma. On the roundabout."

"Not Euniss?"

"No. Did you?"

"I thought I did."

"Was she with Ernie or the gas-meter man?"

('She was with your horrible Richard,' a voice said in Liz's head.) "Perhaps I didn't see her after all," she said.

"A film I remember," Arthur was saying to Mr Beddoes, "although it was all tommy-rot, of course, was *Romance*. With Greta Garbo."

CHAPTER THIRTEEN

FIRST, RICHARD must choose the house. All the
afternoon, he walked round the outskirts of the town.
At last he found it—crumbling lavender stucco, an
iron-work balcony. It looked a house with a past, but
no future. In the little front garden, the earth was hard
and sour under dusty laurels; lace curtains dyed mauve
hung crookedly at the long windows. 'Hollybank' was
in gold letters on the fanlight: but there was no holly, no
bank. A house that had come down in the world, he
thought.

He walked on slowly, the afternoon sun very hot on
his shoulders. In his imagination, he walked about
inside that house, sat his mother down in the drawing-
room, stood a different, fiercer father by the fireplace.
A terrified maid smashed crockery in the basement. He
himself, a little boy, hid under the laurel bushes,
clutching a dog, too scared to go indoors: but he could
see his mother through the windows; she put up her
beautiful, frail hands over her tired face and bowed her
head.

He turned round and walked back. The house,
which had perhaps once stood in a larger garden, was
wedged in now between a garage and a little placarded

newspaper-shop. He went into the shop to ask for cigarettes. A woman came through from a room behind the shop, drying her hands on a tea-cloth. There was a smell of onions.

"Forgive me asking," he began. "I wonder if you can help me."

"Turn that gas off!" she shouted back into the little room. "What do you want?" She let her dull eyes rest upon him.

"I wonder . . . have you been in the district long?"

"Two years."

"Do you know anything about the people in the next house?"

"I can't say I do."

She put her hand on the door of the back room and looked measuringly at him.

"Have they been there long?"

"I couldn't say."

"It was my home when I was a boy. I got a fancy to see it again."

"Well, that's up to you."

"Are they the sort of people who'd object?"

"Are you a detective?"

"A detective? Good God no!" He laughed reassuringly.

"Well, hop it then. See."

She opened the door of the room behind her, but stood waiting for him to leave the shop.

Outside, he lit a cigarette and strolled past the house, throwing the match through the iron railings.

He felt curiosity now, above all other feelings.

'Hollybank. Vale Terrace', he repeated to himself and he began to walk back to his hotel, going carefully along, avoiding the cracks between the paving-stones.

Beyond the swing-door of the Griffin, he met Morland Beddoes on his way out. He would have passed him by without speaking, but Morland stopped to praise the weather.

"And did you enjoy the Fair last night?" he continued, as Richard moved away.

"Oh, the Fair!" Richard smiled condescendingly, but his heart hammered as he went upstairs.

He sat down on the edge of his bed and there was a knocking sound in his head. Each time Morland tried to start a conversation with him he felt menaced. He remembered the question the woman in the newspaper-shop had asked him. Yes, he wished he were a detective: it would be an easy excitement, like fox-hunting: the gradual narrowing down, taking one's time, playing with the prey, in conversations about the weather, polite enquiries; making some other man sit on his bed with his head banging, his shirt cool with sweat.

He crooked his legs up and in one movement lay on his back on the bed, staring up at the ceiling. His world passed before him upon the yellowing, cracked and rather cobwebbed expanse, not a continuous unfolding as before a drowning man's eyes, but in a jerking series of pictures, clicking into place, assembled quickly like a kaleidoscope, or What The Butler Saw. He could not, when he was tired as now, differentiate between the real and the imaginary, and he did not connect the pictures in his mind, nor draw conclusions from them. So the scene of his mother and father opening his letter in the jazzy, *démodé* little sitting-room he hated so much was succeeded by a different mother and father, of a higher social standing, ensconced in the sad and faded elegance of Hollybank, watched through the window by himself as a little boy. The first picture was cheerful, highly-coloured, all orange and lemon; the other washed delicately in with violet and indigo and grey. In the first, was the father who was proud of his son for all the things the son despised—the scholarship to the secondary-school, the sergeant's stripes; the mother who fussed over his material condition and rode rough-shod over his aspirations with her cosiness: then the pale and tragic picture he had invented—the brutal and sadistic father, the broken, lovely, haunted mother, romantic, as only the dead can be. He did not know which was real. He had always told lies, always invented sources of self-pity. If he had an audience, he was saved. When he was alone, he was afraid. He had banished reality and now it was as if he were only reflected back from the mirrors of other people's minds.

And he was frightened of Mr Beddoes. He felt him to be more than a match for him, with his quiet waiting game. But he would escape him. In two days, three days, he would slip away. And tonight the thought of meeting Camilla offered a temporary safety.

'I won't take her to that house,' he suddenly decided. 'But somewhere quiet, where we can talk. I'll drop all that game and tell her the truth instead. I'll shut my eyes fast and go on through the whole story, unhurried and monotonous, the flat, undaunted and intolerable truth. As if she were my diary. It will be a great burden to lay down. A wonderful relief. In all the world, who else would listen to me; who else would hear me to the end?'

.   .   .   .

"I want to show you a house. The house I lived in as a boy. Drink that up and come with me."

"Why this evening?" Camilla asked, putting down her empty glass.

"It's a special day. My mother's birthday. Goodnight, George."

"Good-evening, sir. Good-evening, madam."

"I'm not sure that I approve of all this harking back," Camilla said, out on the pavement. "Which way?"

"Along here."

They set off with the sun in their eyes.

"My book stirs it all up," he said.

"You are making a myth out of your childhood, a kind of legend out of your mother."

"*Your* mother's still alive."

"Yes, she's certainly alive. And ah so busy. Domineering other women on committees, but being submissive in the home. I've failed, of course, because I have no man to devote my life to. But my brothers, she implies, have done well to escape that devotion."

"You should **marry** me," he said.

If this were not irrelevant, it was insulting, she decided.

"Why don't you?"

"I've told you. I'm not in love with you, and I don't approve of the way you live."

"I learnt it in the war."

"The war's over now."

"I've promised you, I'll stop. I'm going to . . . I'm going up North, to Edinburgh. To please you, I would even grovel to my father for money to see me through."

"It is absurd not to borrow it from me."

He made no answer.

"How are you going to get your luggage out?" she asked. She had begun to wonder this in the middle of the night.

"You must leave it to me. It's the sort of thing I can do—the spice of life."

"I shan't ever know what happens to you." She looked away, her slanting, embarrassed glance. Because he said nothing, she was obliged to go on. "Shall you write to me?"

"I'm not very good at putting pen to paper," he said cruelly.

"A fine thing for a writer to say."

"Of course I shall write to you."

'Next term!' she thought. She would read the letters by the gas-fire in the bed-sitting room.

"How far is this house?"

"Not very far."

'It is true,' she thought. 'I hate him and desire him. I mock him, I chide him, I despise him, but all my body shakes at his touch, and when he goes away I shall despair.'

A little breeze swirled dust along at their feet. The street was quiet.

"Here it is!" he said.

He knew at once that he had been clever in choosing his house; for she stopped, her face grew intent, her eyes narrowed dreamily. He took her arm and drew her closer to him. They stood together on the pavement, and looked up at the dusty windows.

"Yes," she said softly. "I can imagine it all going on inside such a house."

"It was a different house then."

"Of course."

He seemed dreadfully struck with animation, as if only the past vivified him.

"Let us knock on the door and ask the way somewhere," she suggested. "It would give us a peep into the hall."

"If someone came to your house and asked to look inside it because they once lived there, would you refuse?" he asked her.

"No. Of course, I shouldn't."

"Then let us ask it."

"Good heavens no! They might be most put out."

"Why think so much worse of other people, than of yourself?" he asked.

"*You* go!"

"I want you to see."

"Very well. But if he—she—is cross, I shall take to my heels and run."

The gate was tipped with cast-iron fleur-de-lys; it groaned as they pushed it open. Brown and yellow broken tiles led to the front door.

"Hollybank," she murmured, her eyes on the fan-light.

He drew out a rusty bell which jangled through the house.

"I'm afraid," she whispered. There was goose-flesh on her arms, although it was a warm evening. "There's no one in."

But footsteps echoed along a tiled hall, a profile appeared against the dark blue and garnet glass panel.

What most dismayed Camilla, appeared to give Richard confidence.

The woman's face looked grey against her brassy hair which was mole-coloured near her scalp. Her neck-line went diving down in a vain attempt to reveal her bosom; a gold cross hung above. Just as Camilla was preparing for flight, Richard launched into his story.

"Why not?" the woman said kindly. "Step inside and excuse the mess, won't you?"

Richard clasped Camilla's hand firmly.

"I wanted to bring my fiancée," he was saying, having discarded the explanation about writing his autobiography.

The smell was suffocating. Cats had wetted the

carpets for centuries, Camilla decided. Bushels of onions had been fried. No one had washed, or opened a window. A perambulator stood on one side of the hall-stand, a bicycle on the other.

"Where d'you want to start?" the woman asked, throwing open doors hospitably. "We haven't been here very long ourselves. Only the twelve-month."

Impossible, in a year, to heap so much litter into a house, Camilla thought, trying not to have any expression on her face.

"Grandma, here's a gentleman who used to live here."

An old woman, who had seemed to be a mound of rusty clothes, stirred and lifted her head. Her hands lay on her lap as if they were separate from her body, two little sleeping animals. Behind her, french windows opened on to a verandah. The frail beauty of the room, with its fine proportions, its round-topped windows, was no longer to be seen, so much distracted the eye, so many ornaments, so much odd and disintegrating furniture, so many photographs of children with teddy-bears and white socks.

"My mother used to sit there just as you are," Richard said to the old lady. He went across the room and looked into the garden. One or two laurel bushes did indeed grow in the beaten earth, but nothing else. For the rest, the garden was decorated with buckled-up bed-ends and a row of napkins.

'It must break his heart,' Camilla thought.

The old woman said nothing. She stared before her,

propped up in her chair, inanimate. 'It is what is called the evening of her life,' Camilla decided in disgust.

"You must take a peep upstairs," the younger woman was saying.

"Oh, no, we have troubled you too much . . ." Camilla protested.

"No trouble. So long as you excuse the muddle. We're a bit upside-down today."

'And tomorrow and tomorrow . . .' Camilla thought, and Richard took her hand again and led her from the room.

On the half-landing they met a girl on her way down. So polished, so clean was she, so dazzling-white in her linen frock, that it was difficult to imagine her emerging from a room in that house, or even going down the staircase without getting soiled. She smelt sweet, she tinkled softly with bracelets, a fine gold chain was clasped round her bare brown ankle above her white shoe.

"Going out, Margie?" the other woman asked her.

"I'm late."

She looked without curiosity at Richard and Camilla and disappeared downstairs.

"My sister," the woman said. As she went on upstairs in front of them, yellowed heels were lifted out of her feathered slippers. "This is her room. She won't mind."

The same litter. Clothes cascaded out of drawers, powder was white over the furniture and the mirrors, shoes across the floor.

"And this is mine and Grannie's. Oh, pardon, I've forgot to make the bed."

Camilla stood in the passage, but caught a glimpse in the wardrobe-mirror of a large orange cat asleep on some rumpled bedclothes. 'His mother's room, I daresay,' she thought.

Stair-carpet changed to linoleum on the next flight of stairs. Outside the landing window were two cowls turning slowly.

"Oh, I remember!" he cried. "They frightened me so when I was little. I was scared to come past this window as it grew dark. I thought they were two nuns."

"My kiddies say the same," the woman agreed.

In the room Richard decided to claim as once his own, three children lay asleep. "Doreen, Joycie, Ivor," their mother introduced them.

"We shall disturb them," Camilla whispered, drawing back on to the landing.

"I like to pop up to see if they're all right. I'm always up and downstairs to them. I love children."

"They are all yours?"

"Doreen's my sister's really."

Camilla murmured.

"Yes, I love children. Sometimes I come up at night and take a look at them, and I think to myself 'I wonder what I should do, if I came in one morning and found them lying there dead'."

"You mustn't think things like that," Camilla said robustly.

"There's no stopping me, I'm afraid," she said with pride. "But I don't want any more. I said to Grandma, 'Grandma I've had my whack. If I fall again, I throw myself in the river.' I mustn't depress you though, just engaged. I was three days in labour with Ivor. I'm small, of course. Yes, ever so small."

Richard came out of the bedroom and joined them.

"The doctor I had to Ivor said to me 'You're exceptionally small, Mrs Mortimer. Really made more like a girl of twelve. You'll never have an easy time.' Margie's different. Seen all you want to?" she asked pleasantly. "I won't ask you down in the basement, if you'll excuse me. We're in rather a pickle down there."

"It's been very kind of you."

"Not at all. I like a chat. I don't see much company. Not like Margie. Come and have a drink with Grandma, won't you?"

"We must go . . ." Richard began, but he stopped by the landing window and stared out. "It's queer and disturbing . . . those nuns. And the virginia-creeper on the wall. I used to unstick it from this sill. It all seems so far away, like another world."

He felt the two women watching him. Camilla looked away first. The other had tears in her eyes. He suddenly wished that Camilla was not there. And because he knew she wanted to escape, he allowed himself to be urged into the room where Grandma sat, and watched while crème-de-menthe was poured out into some fancy tumblers. Grandma drank hers calmly as if it were milk, and put the glass aside.

"Yes, it's a lovely colour," her grand-daughter agreed, sipping and holding the smeared glass against the light.

Camilla put her lips to it reluctantly—the dirty tumbler, the sticky scalding sweetness.

Richard's manner, she could not help observing, was slightly tinged with flirtation toward this frightening woman. The evening was like a nightmare to her, in every way, and she stood nervously beside him, full of impatience and distress.

When at last they were waved away, she took the outside air into her lungs greedily, as if it would cleanse them. He walked away from the house without speaking, and once looked back.

"That was dreadful for you," she said at last.

"Dreadful?"

"To see your mother's house, her room . . ."

"It was so different—only bits reminded me . . ."

"It was silly to go. It is always silly to do that sort of thing. Painful and depressing."

"I couldn't resist it."

"That dreadful woman too," she said wearily.

"I'm sorry about it. Forgive me."

"Let us go somewhere and forget it. Somewhere quiet. And clean."

.   .   .   .

Liz was bored with the evening before it started. 'Why does it seem so dull?' she wondered, 'so different from other years?' What had most checked her happiness or altered her viewpoint; marriage, or child-birth, or her broken friendship?

'People change,' she thought, looking out of the window above the sink where she was doing Harry's washing. 'They change from year to year, and from place to place, and it always is a great blow in the breast to find one's friends have altered as much as one has oneself; especially if it is not along the same lines.'

She rinsed out the napkins and carried them to the clothes-line. Camilla had gone out; Frances was still painting. The evening yawned at her, timeless, empty. Hotchkiss lay outside the kitchen-door asleep. Each time his side went down, his ribs stuck out like a hay-rake.

She wandered back through the house, peeped at Harry, tidied the bedroom. "Thomas Aquinas," she read aloud, picking up a new book from beside Camilla's bed. She looked inside it, but it was all about nothing, like Arthur's books. Very sketchily, she brushed her hair and put on the ring Frances had given her.

'I could pick her some flowers,' she suddenly thought, an idea, not new, but linked with her childhood, with the great bunches of varnished buttercups she had gathered for Frances in the park, the long wilting sheaves of sorrel and moon-daisies, the warm handfuls of primroses. 'But flowers in August are so dull,' she thought, wandering listlessly downstairs and standing in the porch, surveying the parched garden.

'There she is!' Morland thought, opening the gate, catching her unawares. 'Poor Liz, with all her thoughts upon her face.'

"You look dejected."

"Flowers in August are so dull," she repeated aloud.

"I like the rose-coloured zinnias," was the most he could say. "Where is Frances?"

"Still working. I was thinking I should do a great flower-piece for the parlour, for a surprise."

"Let us do it together," he suggested.

"If you like. There is a nice large tureen we could arrange them in . . ."

"Where are some secateurs?"

"Secateurs? Oh, I just *pick* flowers." She thought him a bit old-maidish. "Sometimes I pull so hard the roots come up but I just tread them back," she said, to shock him.

"What colours shall we eliminate?" he asked, after he had been shocked.

"I think red and orange," she said, for these were the only colours she could see.

"Here are some secateurs!" he said, rummaging in the porch. "I think we'll have yellows and white and some straw-coloured grasses."

"I mustn't go out of the garden," she said, feeling that the flower-piece wasn't going to be hers any more. "I have to listen for Harry."

"Just a little way along the lane, I saw some Queen Anne's Lace."

"What's that?" Although she knew.

"I shall show you, sweet Cockney."

She laughed, because she was never cross for long.

"What is Frances painting? Do you know?" he asked in a low voice, stooping to snip off some white sweetpeas.

"I don't know. She might have a stark-naked Hottentot down there as a model, the way she shuts me out."

She sat down on the doorstep and watched him picking the flowers. 'Arthur wouldn't fuss about with that,' she thought.

"I feel I have known you many years," he said.

"Why?"

"I've looked at you so much. Hanging above my fireplace."

"Oh, I don't think *that* looks in the least like me," she said aloofly.

"What were you thinking? I have often wondered."

She picked a leaf and began to strip it down to the veins. "You see, I go for long stretches without thinking anything. Mooning, Arthur calls it. What did you think of Arthur?"

This question did not appear to shock him.

"He would always do good to his fellow-men," he said cautiously, cutting a flower he didn't want.

"Camilla would say he does too much good to his fellow-women," Liz said, laughing.

"Why should Camilla say that?" he asked gravely.

"She dislikes him."

"That must be a grief to you."

"I don't have griefs, only impatiences," she said modestly.

"Come along the lane and gather some grasses."

"No. I'll wait here," she said, laziness, not mother-love, prompting her. Yet when he had disappeared, she found that she was waiting for him to return, and was glad to see him coming in at the gate again. He seemed to have left her to collect not only wild-flowers and grasses, but resolution as well, for he came straight up to the porch and sat down beside her on the door-step, crumpled, worried, kindly.

"Where is Camilla this evening?"

"Gone out," she said flatly.

Not in the least baulked, he asked: "Have you any idea where she goes?"

"Yes."

"And whom she meets?"

"Yes."

"The man you saw at the Fair last night."

"How do you know I saw him?"

"You pretended too hard that you did not."

"I didn't want Camilla to see him. Under the circumstances."

"What sort of a delusion is it she has?"

"I don't understand," she said untruthfully; and then: "He is very handsome, you know."

"How long has she known him?"

"A week. She met him on the train coming here."

"He is not to be trusted, you know.'

"No men are," she said blandly.

203

Quite simply, he said: "I am to be trusted," and she knew at once that it was so. "I haven't much character, and so my temptations to betray others are not like most people's. I'm a spectator. Nothing much comes my way but other people's confidences, and now I am used to listening and being quiet about what I hear."

"Nothing much comes Camilla's way either."

"I have a sense of fear for her, an idea that I should not let her out of my sight."

"What do you know about that man, then?"

"I think he has delusions of grandeur. For one thing he's not and never was a Group-Captain as he signed the hotel-register. Then . . . he's a menace to women," he added.

Liz laughed uncomfortably. "Oh, Camilla's not a young girl, you know."

"She's more at his mercy than most young girls would be."

She shifted uneasily. "I can't do anything," she said. "We are somehow estranged." She stood up and put her hand down to pull him to his feet. "Are you fond of her?" she asked shyly.

"Fond? I don't know."

"I wish you were," she said.

.   .   .   .   .

"I haven't a clean shirt even," Richard said pettishly, looking at his cuffs with disgust.

"I could wash some for you," Camilla offered.

"Could you, sweetheart? And what would those women say to that?"

"I no longer care. In three days I suppose you'll be gone, and I shan't see you again."

"Come with me."

"I have my own life." Very boldly she took his hand and examined the great scar across the palm. "And you don't really want me," she whispered.

"Your scruples might be a liability," he agreed.

"In that house . . . why did you say I was your fiancée?"

"A game I was playing. I liked pretending it."

"But why?"

"I do like pretending things."

"Yes, I know. In the end, you won't know what's real . . ."

"That may be as well."

"Why are you so frightened?"

"I'll tell you another day. Tomorrow."

"Tomorrow? You won't see me tomorrow."

"I must."

"You see, we have a picnic up here in the Clumps. Every year they have it, Frances and Liz, perhaps Liz's husband. I couldn't not go to it. They wouldn't forgive it."

"Wait till I've gone!"

"I can't ask them that. They don't know about you."

"1 must see you tomorrow."

"Why?"

She put his hand to her cheek and shut her eyes, feeling that she talked at random. The little breeze there had been all the evening lifted her hair, turned the white leaves of the wayfaring-trees which grew about the chalky hill.

"Why must you see me tomorrow?" she insisted.

"Something I have to tell you."

"Tell me now."

"I can't tonight. I started off wrong."

"What do you mean?"

"All that about the house, and my mother, got in the way."

He lay flat down on the turf, his forehead resting on his arm, and his mouth drooped like a sulky child's.

"Now you're unhappy!" she cried in despair. "You weren't so unhappy at the time."

"If my mother had seen . . ."

"I know, but she didn't. It doesn't touch her. And nothing's changed."

"I can't tell what is real any longer."

She took his head in her lap and tried to comfort him, although she felt that he was indulging a fantastic grief.

At last: "I am real," she said diffidently. It had taken all her courage, and he did not seem to hear.

.   .   .   .   .

The flower-piece looked very fine in the lamplight. Each petal lay alongside the next according to plan. It was a great work of art, Frances told them; and they felt like praised children as they drank their coffee. But their pleasure was overlaid by anxiety for her. She had come up to the cottage, looking tired and ill, and now sat nursing her elbow, while her coffee grew cold beside her.

Moths blundered about the lampshade, and she watched them, not stirring in her chair. Morland did everything for her, hung up her overall, put a shawl round her shoulders.

"Where is Camilla?" she asked, groping for her coffee-cup. Morland leant over and put it into her left hand.

"I am here," Camilla said at the door.

"Coffee, Cam dear?" Liz began, jumping up and scuttling about, as if there was some awkwardness to cover.

"No work tomorrow," Morland reminded Frances. "There is our picnic, don't forget."

"I've no energy left for picnics."

"I've set my heart on this."

"I think it will rain tomorrow," Camilla said, sitting down in the lamplight. They were all silent, until Morland said: "The swifts were flying too high for rain."

He and Camilla looked at one another. Then she shrugged her shoulders.

'They are all watching me,' she thought.

"Darling, let me see you to bed," Liz said. She knelt down at Frances's feet and clasped her hands over her knees. "I'll brush your hair for you: And bring you some warm milk. It will be round that way for once. Please!"

For the first time that she could ever remember, Frances wanted to lean on someone else. If she consented, she felt that it would mean the end of independence: once she let Liz do for her anything more than that which respect for an older woman dictated—and which was meet and proper, she believed—she saw a danger of slipping too easily into utter helplessness. She struggled for a moment, then she said quietly: "Very well, my dear. Thank you," and let Liz draw her to her feet.

But once upstairs, she found her about as helpful as a little girl playing at nurses; enthusiastic, but quite incompetent. She fetched so many things which were not wanted, blundering about the room in an excess of willingness, and while she was brushing her hair, suddenly conceived such a brilliant idea that she knocked Frances's head quite hard with the side of the hair-brush.

"Oh, hell! Oh, dear, forgive me. I did have such a wonderful idea about the future. You know how I worry about you being here alone. But why should you any more, winter after winter, when you could live quite safe and sound with me? It isn't so bad there, and Arthur adores you. You *should* come. It would help me. I could deal with Mrs Taylor better if you were there, and her sadness, and I should behave better, so that Arthur would love me more. Then we should all be happier, and you wouldn't be so lonely."

Frances looked steadily down into her lap. "I'm not lonely," she said. "But you're a good girl, my dear."

.   .   .   .

Downstairs, Morland and Camilla faced one another awkwardly across the flowers.

"You're tired," he said briefly, hoping to begin the conversation.

She knocked a great furry-legged moth away from her cheek, with a look of unutterable disgust.

"My feet ache," she agreed, as unemotional as she could sound.

"When this holiday of yours is over, will you one day have lunch with me in London?"

"Yes please," she said dully.

"We could go to the Ballet perhaps," he suggested.

"That would be very nice." ('Nice and remote,' she thought.)

She put out her hand to the flowers they had so carefully arranged and pulled off one or two leaves. He looked away.

"Unless there is anything you prefer," he said.

Her nervous fingers stripped and twisted the flowers, shredded the petals. He had not the heart to stop her.

"Prefer to what?" she asked, looking blankly at him through the foliage.

"To the Ballet."

"Oh, I'm sorry. No. Nothing."

She snapped a twig precisely in half, and with a tremendous effort pulled herself to and said: "I am very fond of Ballet. . . . As a matter of fact," she added.

Liz came in quickly and her mouth opened when she saw their flower-piece, their evening's work, their praise-earner, so scattered and unkempt, but the briefest look from Morland kept her silent, and she shut her mouth again. Camilla picked up her coffee-cup and began to drink without lifting her head.

"I must start my long walk home," said Morland.

CHAPTER FOURTEEN

"Yes, Arthur has come!" Liz shouted back into the room. "So we can go in the car after all. Oh, I am so pleased that you came!" she cried, running across the lawn to meet him. "Now we can all go in the car. It will be so much better than the bus."

"I am glad to be so useful."

"How nice you look," she said soothingly.

In the kitchen Mrs Parsons was cutting sandwiches. Camilla was feeding the trimmings to Hotchkiss, who let them drop out of his mouth on to the kitchen floor. She did not know how much this was annoying Mrs Parsons.

"Good-morning, Camilla!" Arthur said, as he came in at the back door.

"Good-morning, Arthur!" She bowed, sitting on a corner of the table, swinging her legs.

'The heighth of bad manners!' Mrs Parsons thought. 'She can't even get to her feet when a gentleman comes into the room.'

Frances slit open a long thin loaf and into it slipped a folded omelette, beautifully billowy at the edges and flecked with green.

The kitchen was very warm already, at not yet

eleven o'clock, and smelt of chives and coffee and methylated spirit.

'Why they must all congregate in here,' Mrs Parsons thought—for there they were: Arthur leaning against the dresser, Camilla perched on the table, Frances at the stove, Liz at the sink. Under the table, Hotchkiss lay among the crusts of bread and bits of lettuce. 'Especially,' Mrs Parsons was thinking, 'on a morning when I have such a lot to say to madam.' Coming up the lane, she had walked quickly, overflowing with all she had to impart—Ernie docile at last and the wedding fixed; Euniss intent on hiring a bridal-gown from one of the film-studios; refusing to be married at the chapel, saying she must go all the way to Torquay for her honeymoon although her sickness in the mornings would make any travelling a hazard; setting her heart on a dusty-pink two-piece for going away; insisting on a new navy suit for Ernie, and gloves, and for her father too although all he would run to was a good tanning of her backside, he had said.

"And where are you to live after this fine wedding, miss?" her mother had enquired.

"I couldn't care less," she had said, plucking her eyebrows at the mirror over the sink.

"And what about the baby-clothes?"

"And what about them?" she had yawned.

All this Mrs Parsons wanted to unburden upon Frances, otherwise it would be another week, and so much happening between one Saturday and the next. But they all perched about gossiping, and now Camilla began to pour out coffee, moving Arthur so that she could reach the cups on the hooks behind him.

"Who is reading St Thomas Aquinas?" he asked, picking up a book from the window-sill.

Camilla flushed.

"I didn't know you were a Thomist," he said, seeming to weigh the book in his hand. His voice was dry and mocking.

"How could you?" she asked lightly. "How could you, indeed, know anything about me?"

'Sarky!' Mrs Parsons thought.

"What's this on Harry's neck?" Liz asked, coming in with the baby. She handed him to Arthur and a long string of dribble attached itself to his jacket.

She fluffed up the fine hair at the back of his neck, and the skin underneath was faintly mottled.

"What is it?"

"That's a teething-rash, madam," Mrs Parsons said, drawn irresistibly away from her sandwich-cutting. "Acidulation," she added certainly.

Camilla drew in her cheeks, glancing at Arthur.

"There's one cure for that," Mrs Parsons said. "That's fasting-spittle."

"What's fasting-spittle?" asked Liz.

"In the morning, madam, as soon as you wake up, just give your hand a good lick and put it to the baby's neck. The poison that's collected in your mouth all night will kill the rash. Mr Parsons will tell you he cured his chilblains for good that way and that alone. But first thing in the morning, remember. There's not the same poison in the spit during the day."

"Then I must wait until tomorrow," Liz said politely.

Arthur was interested to see a new side of his wife, and admired her nice gravity. Camilla choked over her cup of coffee.

At this moment, Morland arrived, looking very hot in a navy-blue suit. Arthur, in alpaca, was most cordial to him. He made several clergymen's jokes about having been one man among so many ladies, he feigned relief, was both gallant and manly. Mrs Parsons at once went over to the side of Lady Davidson and other ladies of his parish, in admiration of how he always struck the right note. Liz looked doubtfully at Morland above the baby's head. Camilla coughed still, her hand on her bosom, her face pink.

Frances seemed wrapped up this morning in a cocoon of silence, of preoccupation. She had wanted to go on with her painting, so the day was a day slipped out of the rest and thrown away. 'My work is my love,' she thought. 'My consolation, and refuge. In the midst of other people, against the thought of death, of war, I turn the secret page in my own mind, knowing that though I seem to have less than others, in reality I have more than ever I bargained for.'

She went out into the garden to pick tomatoes, a paper bag in her hand. Hotchkiss lumbered after. The tomatoes were warm in the sun. She turned each one carefully, almost unscrewing it from its plant, and as she picked them freed their lovely sharp fragrance.

It was a pearly morning; the sky, which had been cloudless for days, had flocks of little clouds across it, like a sky painted on a ceiling; but still the sun dazzled, the red ants like garnets ran in the parched grass.

'It *has* been a nice life,' she reassured herself, as she filled the paper bag. She pinched up some lemon-balm and held her scented hand to her face. 'I *did* always do what seemed right to me at the moment. I *was* happy. I never consciously spared myself or kept anything meanly back, and when I die, I'll know I spent it all, the life I was given. And the great happiness I have over Liz, bringing her up and loving her, could not have been more intense if I had been her own mother. Yet I was too self-sufficient, as if I evaded the pain and the delight of human-relationships, which I never did knowingly. But if I was ever gravely at fault, I was at fault over that. For even Liz's marriage is better than no marriage at all.'

"Are you better this morning?" Morland asked. He had come down the path and she had not noticed him. "Are you rested?" He took the bag of tomatoes from her, as if he must relieve her of the intolerable burden.

"Yes, I am quite rested," she said, and she twisted a yellow rose off an archway and put it in his buttonhole. She had never done such a thing in her life, and felt so reckless that she smiled at herself.

"When can I see your painting?" he asked.

"Oh, later, later," she assured him. "When it is done."

"Tell me about it."

215

"I let the devil tempt me after all." She walked a little ahead of him down the path.

"You came out of that tulgy wood?"

"You shall see."

Liz and Arthur came out of the kitchen door carrying baskets to the car. Camilla followed with the baby, trying to seem unconcerned. Arthur's car was not large, and Morland at once offered to go by bus.

"No, *I* shall go by bus," Camilla insisted. "I know a short cut up the hill."

"We'll go by bus together then," Morland suggested.

"That leaves only three of us in the car, which is rather absurd," said Arthur, who did not like having such a small car, nor being reminded of it.

"I can easily go alone," Camilla insisted.

"Cam and I could go together," Liz suggested. "It will be like the old days." Arthur looked stonily ahead. "Frances can take Harry on her lap."

"There is no question of it," Morland said. "I am going to go by bus, and I am going alone, and I shall really enjoy it quite well and shall be there almost as soon as you."

'Because I am a clergyman, he thinks I drive like an old woman,' Arthur thought. "Perhaps Elizabeth should drive," he said aloud, "and I will walk with Beddoes."

'He was Morland a few moments ago,' thought Liz.

Mrs Parsons came running out with a thermos-flask which had been left on the dresser.

'Gentry take their pleasures sadly,' she thought,

remembering the crates of beer loaded on to the chara before the Darts Team Outing set off for Southend, or Hindhead, or Bognor Regis.

"We haven't settled much," Arthur said sharply, standing with one hand on the car-door. For all this, he had given up a tennis-party at Lady Davidson's.

"We have settled everything," said Morland.

Frances climbed into the back of the shaky little car and sat down.

"There is room for all of us," she said. "Morland, will you go in front, please, and take the baskets on your knee? The three of us will be very comfortable in the back with the baby."

They did as they were told.

"It wants the self-starter not to work now," Arthur said in a slipshod English which betrayed his irritability. But the car, at least, behaved well, and soon they were going smoothly along the hedged lanes, each wrapped away in private thoughts, in secret daydreams.

Arthur drove fast, but very well; and, as he drove, his spirits lifted. He began to sing to himself and once said over his shoulder to Morland: "An absurd car this. Like a little tin-bath." He felt mellow with happiness.

"I haven't a car," said Morland. "And if I had I wouldn't know how to drive it."

The sun was very high now and streamed down upon the valley as if into the calyx of a flower. The leather of the car seats burnt through their thin clothes. Liz and Cam lay back on either side of

Frances; once they glanced at one another and smiled.

But Frances and the baby were fast asleep.

. . . .

The sun seemed to touch their bones, poured into them as if they were hollow like cups. Even the trees below in the valley looked dazed. Nothing moved, but the heat shimmering until the view was like a bad photograph.

"Here we loll, full of food," Camilla said. "Like old seals sunning themselves on a ledge."

A little train plodded along the valley, its smoke at a rakish angle. "It will never get anywhere," Liz said, leaning back on her elbows.

Morland had caught the sun across his forehead and cheek-bones. He had made himself a hat out of his knotted handkerchief and Arthur blamed him silently for looking so absurd, so tripperish.

The stunted wayfaring-trees gave little shade, and Frances had put up a faded grey silk parasol. She sat upright under it and fanned herself with a paper bag.

'Le Déjeuner sur l'Herbe,' Morland suddenly thought. He took his hat off and wiped his mouth with it, to hide his smile.

"We should have climbed higher to the Clumps," Liz said. "It would be cooler there."

"But it is so full of broken bottles and the remains of bonfires," Camilla said.

"Shift Harry again," said Arthur.

Round the tree went Harry, his rug pursuing the moving patch of shade. He looked up into the silvery, dusty leaves and turned his hands ecstatically.

Morland gazed down at the little town. He felt it all at his fingertips, began to see it as the scene for a film— the High Street; the Market Square; the little railway-station with its few moments of confusion and its long lulls; the faded tea-shops and drowsing back-streets; the old gravestones in the churchyard; the Public Gardens.

"It has a life of its own," he said, and he swept his hand across the scene. "It is a corporate thing, with its own atmosphere, its own set of characters. It breeds its own set of characters, as Rouen bred Madame Bovary. I can imagine tragedy down there, and drama. I can imagine an English Madame Bovary and the old ladies in the tea-shops watching her, the men in the pubs lifting their mouths from their mugs as she passes in the street. . . ."

"It is what they call a slice of life," Arthur agreed. "A town like that runs across England from the highest to the lowest. . . ."

"I can imagine," Morland persisted, "someone on the run from the police fretting his time away in one of those pubs—in the pub where I am staying, perhaps."

"Life is good. Life is simple," Frances quoted him mockingly.

"If it were a film, that hotel wouldn't be lying there idle," he said. "If it is."

He built it up in his mind, selecting and rejecting.

The camera nosed along corridors, went like a ghost through closed doors, looked down over the banisters, and out of windows at the cobbled square, glanced over a shoulder at a pen scratching a name in the register, picked up a mirror here, an envelope there.

Then he suddenly pushed it all aside and turned to Frances and smiled.

"Only in your paintings would it be just itself, stay where it is and seem sufficient. In life, in literature, in films, it must move on and change and contain other things."

"Why do you read St Thomas Aquinas?" Arthur asked Camilla in a low voice.

"I try to discover why people believe in God."

"Is it important to you to discover that?"

"No, not very," she said carelessly.

She and Liz were making a flower-chain, their laps full of daisies and scabious and lady's slipper and hare-bells. It grew between their hands.

"I can't think why you said it was going to rain," Morland remarked. "It is a perfect day."

"Yes, it's a lovely day," she agreed. "It's the sort of day people remember as the *end* of something—the last day before the war, the last day of peace, the day the Old Queen died, the end of an era. They look back and say: 'It was perfect weather that summer. There never was weather like it, before or after. We didn't know it was the last day of our happiness, and that it would never be the same again'."

"Yes, my mother used to talk like that about the war before last," Liz said. "As if she were in a novel by Galsworthy."

"It *was* like that," Frances said.

"I was a small child at the seaside," said Arthur. "We were hurried away from Dawlish lest the enemy should land there."

"You are all frightening me," cried Liz. "You make me think something horrible will happen tomorrow."

The flower-chain broke in half.

"This time it will be the other way round," Camilla said. "We shall look back on today and say: 'Little did we know that it was the end of our anxieties, our last day of uncertainty.'"

"People never do say that."

"No, things do go on getting worse," Frances said as placidly as if she had said the opposite.

"Only if you take the short view," Arthur said.

"I take the view of three-score years and ten. As much as I can manage. Or be interested in," she said. "Once I begin taking a longer view there is no line to draw. I find myself back among pterodactyls and forward in the time when human beings are only fossils in the rocks. Or ice," she added vaguely.

"But you care about the future of mankind?" he suggested.

"Not in the least," she said calmly.

"You care about—well, Liz, for instance."

"Elizabeth must look after herself. She's not a child now."

"I've had nearly half my life," Liz said, sighing sharply.

"You have still had less than any of the rest of us," Camilla reminded her. "Arthur is in the prime of life," she added, giving him a little sideways glance, as she mended the flower-chain.

Suddenly a shadow lay over her hands. She looked up at the sky. A little cloud had hidden the sun.

"I was right," she said.

The blue was thickening into lavender as if evening were coming already.

"This curious light," Frances began, and then stopped. She put her parasol away and shaded her eyes with her hand, looking to left and right along the valley. She sighed. 'Oh, it flies away,' she thought, striking her hands together in her lap. 'It can't ever be caught or described. For it is one earth one moment and another earth in a second or two. Life itself is an unfinished sentence, or a few haphazard brush-strokes. Nothing stays. Nothing is completed. I can make nothing whole from it, however small. Pinned down, like a butterfly, it ceases to be itself, just as the butterfly becomes something else; dead, unmoving, its brightness gone. The meaning of a painting is a voice crying out: "I saw it. Before it vanished, it was thus." An honest painting would never be finished; an honest novel would stop in the middle of a sentence. There is no shutting life up in a cage, turning the key with a full-stop, with a stroke of paint.'

"Who shall have this flower-chain?" Liz asked.

"Harry," said Camilla.

"He would eat it," Arthur said quickly.

"We cannot give it to you," Camilla said to him. "It is flowers, not laurels."

"Frances should have it," Morland said.

Carefully, they lifted the chain over her head and dropped it on her shoulders. She sat very upright, her hands still clasped in her lap, and smiled.

"I think we should go," Arthur said. "It does look as if the weather's breaking."

He would be glad to get back to the Vicarage. He had his sermon to prepare.

"I think so, too," said Camilla. She got up stiffly and stood looking down at the town in the valley, and the sun and shadow alternating on the tops of the trees. The voices of the others as they packed up the baskets dropped away from her and she tried to imagine herself in this very place alone with Richard again.

She felt a hand touch her wrist and started violently.

"A cigarette?" Morland asked her, holding out his case.

CHAPTER FIFTEEN

MORLAND WENT back to his hotel. From his bedroom-window, he could see the place where they had picnicked; it was far-off, like a vignette on a title-page; had, in this strange yellowish light, exactly the look of an engraving in an old book.

He flung up the window from the bottom and leant out, his elbows on the sill. A stored warmth rose from the wall below him. Perhaps the changed weather, this withdrawal of brightness from the air, had discouraged him, but the market square, flat and shadowless, had a depressing look, presaged disaster. The drifting people suggested only dark lives spent in the back-rooms of little shops, in the coils of what is sometimes encouragingly called private enterprise; dragged down by daily worries, no vision elated them, no intimacy delighted.

'So we trail from birth to death,' he thought, looking down at the dejected bus queue, the people coming out of the station as if beginning to emerge from an anæsthetic. 'From day to day, we drift along, glance at headlines, dully hope for the best, menaced chiefly by one another, all separate yet without identity.'

A sharp gust of wind lifted a man's hat and bowled it

across the square. Pink, laughing, vexed, he left the bus queue and gave chase. His wife stood looking after him; pink, smiling, and vexed, too, at being so singled out. When he returned to her, they stood closer together and chatted in a relaxed and casual way. After a while, their colour subsided; the little ripple of animation was over; they had forgotten.

'But they had one another; they covered their moment of confusion with one another,' Morland thought. 'They exchanged remarks. Just as after parties married people go back to their own privacy and laugh the evening into some sort of order, find their hearts touched by the same things, their scorn mutual, their judgments similar. But I go home alone,' he thought, 'and the noise of company drains slowly out of my head. The quiet overcomes me and I stretch out my hand for a book; for the party was over as I bade my hostess goodbye, just as that picnic was over for me the moment that I left the others. There is no one with whom to discuss it, no one to join me in unravelling the conversation or to guess at the meanings of mood and innuendo or, even better, to exchange drowsy banalities at bedtime, saying: "Arthur is proud of his son," "Liz is uncertain as a mother," "the food was good," "the sun was hot" and "did you notice the ring she was wearing?"; then to put the room into darkness and turn away from one another, but at the very brink of sleep adding: "Frances was abstracted, I thought . . . and what in the world was all that about St Thomas Aquinas . . .?"'

He lit a cigarette and drew a chair up to the open window. Always a staleness and lassitude hangs over late summer's afternoons; returning home at that hour in that season seems an anti-climax; time hangs heavily and a great yawn widens in one's heart.

He spun the dead match down to the gutter. A man passing half-glanced up. 'I left Camilla out of the bed-time dialogue,' he thought. 'I believe I imagined her as the listening one.'

At this moment, he saw Richard coming out of the station, watched him hesitate, buy an evening paper and stand reading it at the kerb before crossing the road.

'I never knew a man to buy so many newspapers,' Morland decided, and he leant forward a little to get a better view, to take this chance of being unseen to try to analyse what possible hold such a man could have over Camilla. Young men like him, spoilt by despised but doting mothers, ruined by good-looks, were always about the film studios, no panache to distract from their shabbiness, or their lack of talent. He had met them there, met them sponging in bars, half-listened to their everlasting jokes about homosexuality, their lisping innuendo, their anti-semitism, their truckling, their voices raised for famous names, lowered only to decry one another. They find release in war-time, sometimes behave bravely; but, turned adrift in peace, find nothing to cover the emptiness of their hearts; not women, nor drink, nor this endless reading of news-papers, he thought; and at that moment Richard folded his paper and looked straight up from the street and into his eyes. The distance between them did nothing to diminish the flicker of fear both felt and showed, as if a match had spluttered into light upon a scene no shade less terrifying for being expected.

'If ever we come near to seeing the truth, it is in one another's eyes,' Morland thought, for in that quick upward glance Richard had exposed his terror and apprehension, had underlined the uneasiness between them, the sense of which remained now after he had moved out of view under the wall of the building, the passers-by covering the pavement, as the living quickly cover the disappearance of the dead.

'Out of all the crowd—just he and I!'

Morland moved away from the window into the shadow of the room. 'The invisible web which drifted out, attached us to one another, so lightly that we alone knew. The web that drew me to Frances, has also its other strands. Beauty and corruption touch us—at the same time, in the same place. Not separately, as in Frances's pictures, but always the two going hand in hand; our days alternate between them, the truth contains them both. The search for beauty, lays bare ugliness as well.'

He walked about the room and sometimes caught a glimpse of himself in a crooked, bamboo-edged mirror. He stopped and examined this reflection, the familiar expectant face, the flying ends of tie, the rather weak, pale eyes.

The door in the mirrored room opened and over his shoulder he saw Richard standing against the strip of

227

darkness from the corridor outside. He turned round.

Fear, corrosive, palpable, leapt between them. Driven into its last corner, the stag turns for the first time, madly, uselessly aggressive, to face the enemy.

"What do you want?"

"I came to ask *you* that," Richard said. "What the devil it is *you* want?"

"I want nothing from you."

"I dislike being spied on. Since you came here; wherever I went, you've followed me . . ."

"Only in your imagination."

"At the Fair, that time in the churchyard late at night, tracking after me, pretending to read the gravestones; you wait for me on the stairs, stop me in the hall. Now you sit watching me from the window . . ."

"Perhaps you interest me as a character," Morland suggested as coolly as he could. "Perhaps I wonder why you're here, why you must bolster yourself up before barmen, and waiters—and women—with pretence and pretension. But, as you are immediately going to say, it's no affair of mine, and my curiosity would only be forgivable if you menaced anyone."

In the final encounter, the trapped creature is a fearsome, not only a fearful thing. Morland put his hand out and leant on the back of a chair. He felt suddenly defeated and exhausted.

"I want nothing of you," he said.

. . . .

"Arthur, it is my turn to ask a favour of you," Liz said.

228

They moved down the bean-row together and she dropped the beans into the colander he was carrying for her.

"There is no question of 'turns'," he assured her.

"I wish you could stay for supper . . . I wish you needn't go . . . but that is not the favour," she added quickly.

"My love, I wish I could, too, but I must work till midnight as it is."

"You could work here."

"I think not."

He had a great political speech to prepare, his sermon for Sunday evening; must bring books from all sides to reinforce his argument; his study would be heaped with them before he went to bed.

"Well, then," she said, relinquishing him, "the favour is to do with Frances."

He liked to see her brown hands among the leaves, watched all her movements with pleasure until she tore down a great branch of leaves and beans by mistake. Even then, although he frowned, he held back his annoyance.

"I thought it would be so nice if she could come to live with us," she said. (For everything was either 'nice' or 'nasty', as he knew.)

"Frances?"

"Yes."

"But she would never consider it."

"I think she would, you know. Things have changed for her in this last year. She won't paint much more.

She's ill and tired, and she's old now. Until this summer she never seemed to me to change . . ."

"Even if she would come, it would be a great responsibility to take upon ourselves . . ."

"But I don't take on any responsibility about Frances. I already have it, wherever she is. And if she were ever seriously ill . . . or . . . or anything of that kind, then I should like her to be with me, with us I mean."

"She is like a mother to you," he suggested.

He simplified all relationships.

'Only my mother could be that,' Liz thought, but she kept her thought to herself.

Arthur was appalled at the prospect of Frances in the house. She seemed to him eccentric, undependable. The elaborate courtesy he accorded her so willingly on these brief visits could scarcely be expected of him permanently, yet he could think of no other sort of behaviour to take its place.

Liz was looking up at him so anxiously that he put the colander down on the top of the hedge beside him and drew her close.

"If it will make you happy," he said, "then of course I say yes."

He clasped his hands round her neck over her hair. "Women's necks are so frail, I am always afraid their heads will break off. What are you thinking?"

She laughed and looked up and her eyes flashed with tears.

"Something occurred to me. All of a sudden, I

thought marriage *is* an institution. It is a thing we build up, not perfect, but real. I can't express myself," she added lamely, "but it was an important thought, I thought."

Hidden between the bean-row and the hedge, he caught her up and embraced her, his soft kisses over her face and upon her hair. 'She talks so much nonsense,' he thought, 'distracts me with such banalities; but she is sweet; she is so very sweet; in a way no other woman is, even the women whom I most admire.'

And it was as if Lady Davidson had risen, given the signal to the other ladies, and withdrawn.

. . . .

Camilla was sitting at the dressing-table writing a cheque, when Liz came in to feed Harry. She folded it and put it in her pocket and took up her comb: all her movements too careless by half, Liz thought.

"Are you going out?"

"Yes."

Liz put safety-pins in her mouth so that she could not be expected to answer.

Suddenly Camilla turned round and her hands parted in that gesture which means 'I cannot keep it from you—here it is—the truth!' and she said, with some courage: "Liz, do bear with me. It isn't for long . . . tomorrow . . . or the day after . . . he's going away. I shan't see him again, I expect, but the thought of him, the idea of it all, colours my life for the moment, and the promise of having letters from him helps me to face the next term."

Liz took the pins from her mouth and asked: "Are you going to marry him?"

"You know I am not."

"Why are you suddenly so lonely?"

"I feel such utter blankness, the future looks so desolate. No worse for me, I know, than many other women; but you have Harry, and Arthur."

"But you are always scornful of Arthur."

"He has the faults of his sex, but much of the excellence too. And if he is a little proud, and a little self-important, those qualities have good things attached to them. He wouldn't fall below his idea of himself, nor fail to uphold you. He has a solid worth, a steadying influence, and—how lucky!—the virtues that are rewarded on earth as well as in heaven. You are better off in the circle of his life, than on your own for the rest of your days."

"Yes, I have just been thinking that," Liz said. "It will seem strange in a day or two, with Arthur gone, your . . . this Richard gone, and Morland . . ."

"Morland?" Camilla asked in surprise.

"He said he must go in a couple of days. We shall be all on our own again, like other years. And I am so afraid you'll be unhappier than you were before."

"I suppose so. It's odd, but I almost wish Morland were staying."

She stood up and put on her jacket. Liz said: "I do want you to know that I care for you very much, and that I want you to be happy." A pain rose in her throat, then slowly subsided. She was always unsteady with tears; emotion bruised her too easily; she cried over books and in the cinema; at weddings, at processions. She could not say 'Many happy returns of the day', or hear the National Anthem played without her eyes brimming over.

Camilla gave her a little awkward sideways glance, standing with her hands touching the dressing-table.

"I shall have to go," she said.

"Goodbye, then."

"Goodbye, Liz dear."

She shut the door very quietly after her and ran down the stairs.

Liz sat and looked at the dressing-table over her baby's head. A clean piece of blotting-paper with a few words printed across it lay there beside Camilla's pen and cheque-book. Each time she looked away, curiosity drew her glance back again. Presently, she carried the baby across the room and holding him on one arm, still at her breast, quickly put up the sheet of blotting-paper against the light. She could read the name 'Richard Elton Esq' very plainly and having seen what she had feared she glanced over her shoulder guiltily, ashamed of her behaviour and trembling, too, with a presentiment of disaster.

·   ·   ·   ·

Later in the evening Morland arrived. He had walked very slowly along the closed-in lanes towards the cottage. The countryside had a curious intentness as if it were listening; each flower stood still, awaiting the storm; in the fields the cows had gone down on their knees.

Under the hard light, the flint cottages were sharply grey and white, bricks brilliantly red. It looked a primitive landscape with wooden figures standing at doorways watching the sky, or taking down linen from clothes-lines.

Liz was playing the piano, the only scrap of music she could remember from her childhood—*Chanson Triste*, though it was not *triste* at all, only flat and dreary. He walked up the path and leant through the open window. His shadow darkened the room and she turned round, startled.

"Ah, Morland!"

Her hands dropped into her lap.

"You always have your tongue hanging out when you play?" he asked.

"It is a sign that I am trying hard."

"The music was a sign of that."

She closed down the lid of the piano. "You shatter all my dreams," she said, swivelling round on the music-stool and facing him. "The vast hushed audience, the orchestra fading out . . ." her hands spread wide dramatically . . . "and then me, I, galloping away into my solo, white hands going up and down, reflected in the concert grand . . ."

"You go to the cinema too much," he said, leaning on the window-sill, among the cactus plants.

"I especially like the dreamy bits where I gaze at the ceiling and smile to myself; you can't see my hands then, only my shoulders moving . . ." Her eyes swam.

"What are you wearing?" he asked politely.

"I think dark green velvet. Perhaps none of this is very real to you," she suggested.

"Better than real."

"Did you never dream things like that?"

"Different things. Physical danger, and I saving the school sergeant from drowning. He used to go down on his knees and thank me every night before I slept. And sometimes the Cricket Captain clapped his hand on my back, speechless with emotion and admiration. Other times, I was lying in a mortuary with the Headmaster pacing up and down beating his knuckles on his brow, full of dark regrets, but too late. . . ."

"And when you grew up?"

"The same sort of thing . . . Morland saying the right word at the right time, then exit. Middle-of-the-night wit."

He disappeared from the window and came in through the door.

"Really famous people . . ." Liz began, winding herself up and then down on the music-stool . . . "do you think they ever dream foolish scenes like that? The sort I dream—how I wrote a wonderful play and made a speech at the first-night . . ."

"What did you wear?" he asked again.

"White crêpe. . . . Draped." She draped the skirt

235

about her with her hands. "Arthur was in one box, Noel Coward in another. I smiled a little smile at both."

"Ever been a ballerina with baskets of roses going up, and generals standing up in the boxes shouting 'brava'?"

"No. That will do for another time. I wonder if Frances . . . for I suppose that she is famous in a way . . ."

"Where is she this evening?"

"In the shed. . . ."

"And Camilla?"

"Gone out." She looked blankly at him for a second, sensed a profound uneasiness in him and then went on rather lamely: "I wonder if Frances dreams of . . . I can't really imagine what . . ."

"Her work is her dream. Anything else would be a distraction."

Both talked of one thing, were thinking of another.

"No glamour, enchantment?"

"The reality must be such an enchantment, that applause afterwards would be only an echo of it. Artists do indeed inherit the earth."

"They suffer though," Liz said. ('In such a *nice* way,' she thought. It was a suffering she could easily bear for them to have.)

"We all suffer. *They* put it to good account."

"I call it passing the buck," she murmured; then made haste to agree with him. "Oh, yes," she said vaguely, "they work away like beavers and turn the grit into a pearl. And what is so funny about that?" she asked, joining in his laughter.

.   .   .   .

Frances put aside her brush with a feeling of great weariness. She sat down and darkened her eyes with her hands, tired, but not as dejected as she looked. Liz had stopped playing the piano and she could hear talking and, once, a great burst of laughter. She supposed that Morland had come, and at the thought of him looked up at her unfinished picture, trying to take it unawares, as painters do, and failed, as they must always fail.

As she looked at it, panic beat about in her. She had no way to turn. There is no past for an artist. What is done is cast away, good only for the time of its creation. Work is the present and the immediate future; but her immediate future was a blank; the present this half-finished painting.

'The mistake is listening to others,' she told herself. 'One has little enough of one's own, but they will strip it away, with their kindness and their good advice. It is best to turn to no one, to seek to please no one, to paint as if there were only oneself in the world. The pleasure of others is a by-product after all, and if ever the whispering voices are allowed to crowd out the *one* voice, the result is this . . .' She took the picture roughly in her hands, the paint tacky against her palms . . . 'a sort of high-pitched silliness, a terrible silliness.' She stared down at the creamy-pink and

237

yellow picture, half a mirror with reflected hands lifting a wreath of roses, a flash of golden hair. 'It is like Ophelia handing out her flowers,' she thought. 'The last terrible gesture but one.'

As if to rid herself of the sight of it, she took the canvas and leant it with its wet paint to the wall. She would never finish it.

'Yes. Ophelia!' she thought, wiping her fingers on a rag. On the bench lay the wreath of roses she had twisted together the day before. She picked it up, and the petals were soft and dead to touch, and warm from the sunlight. 'I shan't paint again,' she thought. 'It is time to finish.'

She heard footsteps along the gravel and when Morland tapped at the door she went quickly to unlock it.

"Are you still working?"

He looked at her with love and concern as she stood in the doorway still holding the wreath of flowers. Then she smiled and shook her head.

"Liz says your coffee will be cold."

"I'm coming." She turned the key in the lock and dropped it into her pocket.

"What is that for?" he asked, touching the faded garland.

"Oh, it is dead."

He put his arm through hers and they walked up the garden towards the cottage. A large drop of rain fell on the path before them, and the poplar trees by the hedge clattered their leaves in a sudden gust of wind.

.   .   .   ,

'To walk in so curious a light was like swimming under water,' Camilla thought.

When Richard turned and held out his hand, she took it gratefully, for the turf was slithery, the hill steep, and it was her second time of climbing it that day.

The world seemed to fall away from them as they went higher, the landscape widened. Below them, rooks made a commotion over the tops of the trees, and other birds, chalk-white, swooped in great arcs against the darkening sky.

"Gulls," she said, stopping to look up at them. "If it is going to rain . . ."

"It won't be much."

She stooped and unbuckled her sandals so that she could walk barefoot on the grass. He stood watching her.

"What did you do at the picnic?" he asked.

"Oh . . . ate and talked."

"To whom?"

"To . . . why, to the others, of course," she said, looking up in surprise.

"Who went?"

"Liz and her husband and Frances. And the baby, of course. And a friend of Frances's."

They walked along the ridge of the earthworks for a little way and then began to climb again towards the Clumps.

"And what did you do all day?" she asked him.

"I was waiting for you. I knew that you would come. I was afraid to leave the bar."

"All day?" She gave him a little, wry, wife's smile.

"In the afternoon . . . you will despise me for this, I'm afraid."

"Tell me."

"I went back to that house."

She flushed.

"I knew I shouldn't tell you," he said quickly. "I wished everything to be perfect this evening."

"But why did you go?"

"I don't know. I felt drawn back. I took some flowers to that woman as an excuse for calling there again."

"I think she is a harlot," Camilla said in a constrained, defiant voice. "Isn't she?"

He laughed. "Harlot's a very grand word for anything she might be," he said.

"The sister, then."

"You find the idea irresistible," he said. "Women always do."

Now they had climbed to the top of the hill and the great clumps of trees threw out their darkness over them. It was, as Camilla had said before, a dismal place full of charred wood and litter. The boles of the trees erupted with bottles, with bone-white flints and rusty tins. Moss covered the ground, and patches of fine grass.

They sat down to rest. The sky was a mulberry colour now and the trees were strangely lucid against it.

"I can't stay there any longer," Richard said, looking down at the town in the valley.

240

"What has happened?"

"I shall tell you later."

His hand shook as he lit his cigarette.

"I have always lost other people through telling lies," he said. "I am afraid to lose you through telling the truth."

"You are going to lose me anyhow if you go away."

He smoothed her hair back from her forehead. "You know, when I first saw you, I thought you rather plain. I wonder why?"

"It seems so long ago. That horrible afternoon. Such strange things cut across one's tracks."

"Forget it."

"I try to."

"What will you do when I've gone away?"

"For the rest of the holiday I shall sit and read in the garden and take the dog for walks and go down to the Hand and Flowers for a drink in the evenings. . . ." She picked up a large flint and seemed to weigh it as she considered the future. Then she threw it away impatiently. "And after that I'll go home and get ready for next term; distemper my room, perhaps; have other women in for coffee; go to lectures . . . wait for your letters," she added. "At half-term, I shall go to Cambridge for the weekend, to see my mother, and she'll be apologetic about me to all her friends because I have never managed to get married. And I'll become cussed and off-hand, and they'll all say I'm soured and difficult. And so I am."

A large drop of rain splashed on her face and another on her hand.

"It's going to pour," she said, glancing up at the sky.

"Those are heat spots."

They could see the storm gathering over the valley. The discoloured sky was veined suddenly with lightning. The gulls had vanished and the rooks were silent.

"Are you afraid of thunder?" he asked her.

She only laughed.

'No, she would have no womanish fears,' he thought. 'Women who live alone grow out of those things. Or they never grow into them.'

The rain came sharply on the leaves above them and they drew back into shelter. They stood, hand in hand, leaning against a tree, looking down over the valley, which seemed to be boiling, with great clouds of vapour rising.

"What time are you going? Shall I come to see you off?" she asked.

"No."

He frowned: with impatience, she thought.

"Now you're angry again. I never know . . ."

"Shall we go?" he asked roughly.

She looked helplessly out at the rain, and then, without speaking, she knelt down and fastened her sandals and followed him, stumbling over the rough-edged stones and the roots of the trees.

"This is a short cut down the hillside," she said curtly, leading the way along a winding path between the wayfaring trees.

"It's easing up," he observed.

It was doing nothing of the kind. Her sleeves began to cling to her arms, her hair darkened with rain. They walked downhill without speaking. Brown water plaited its way along the sides of the gravelly lane.

"There was a house where we used to get tea," Camilla began. "The Old Vicarage."

"You will scarcely get tea now," he said.

"They might let us shelter."

He said nothing.

"Before we are soaked to the skin," she added.

" 'Soured and difficult'," he repeated quietly. "Yes, I can see what you meant."

'Oh Lord, now we are quarrelling,' she told herself. 'We are going to quarrel away the rest of our time together.'

"There are no weapons you disdain," she observed.

"None."

"And you disarm other people first with your self-pity."

"Here is your old vicarage, I should think."

Iron railings had lurched into nettles, ivy covered the walls and fringed the narrow pointed windows.

"The woman may remember me. I shall ask if we can wait until the rain has stopped."

They walked down the rough path with their heads bent against the warm driving rain. In the porch, broken glass on the ground checked them. Yellow frogs leapt away into the ferns.

"It's empty!" Camilla said. "There's no one here."

She wiped the rain from her eyelashes and looked up at the front of the house. Some of the dirty windows had great stars of broken glass. By the hedge she could see now the 'To Let' notice, leaning among the mauve-flowered brambles. Cabbages seeded among the weeds, lettuces had bolted, standing high, like pagodas; convolvulus climbed over a bush of moss roses.

Richard tried the door, but it was locked. They looked through the windows into bare rooms, stained wallpapers with the pale oblongs where large pictures had hung. Cobwebs draped each corner, fireplaces were strewn with the ashes of some long-ago fires.

They walked round to the back, keeping close to the sides of the walls. Moss grew in the drains, groundsel in the brick path. The kitchen door was unlocked and they went in.

"I wonder what happened," Camilla said, and her voice ran round the walls.

A calendar of the year before hung on the back of the door, but the house might have been empty for generations. A great spider sat in the sink, the tracks of slugs silvered the stone floor.

In the hall, he said: "Let us pretend we are married to one another and coming to live here in this house."

She put her hand on the newel of the banisters and looked up the winding stairs.

"It would invite disaster to live in a house like this. I never came inside it before. We used to have tea under a walnut tree in the garden—rustic work table and chairs, tablecloth flapping, little spiders coming down on long threads out of the branches . . ."

He was not listening. He was walking from one room to another, leaving wet footprints over the floorboards; each room echoed to the ceiling as he trod about. He came back into the dark hall.

"What is wrong?" she asked him.

"Let us see upstairs." With his foot on the bottom step, he turned suddenly and took her in his arms. "I am sorry about this," he said, smoothing her wet hair. "And I am sorry for all the hurtful things I ever said to you."

"It doesn't matter."

"I love you."

"I don't think so. But that doesn't matter either."

"Why did you ask me what was wrong? In what way? What did you mean?"

"I thought you seemed restless and unhappy again."

"But *you* quieten me, cover my nerves. Let's go upstairs."

"What was that noise?" she whispered.

"Only thunder."

"It sounded like someone moving furniture about on the bare floors. What would happen if anyone came?"

She went slowly upstairs in front of him, a little afraid. Rain swept across the landing window. The banisters were coated with dust.

At the turn of the stairs, he came close behind her, and put his hands round her waist. Fear leapt through her at his touch. She stopped and turned round, her hand clutching the banisters. She could feel sweat breaking out over her body.

"I don't want to go any farther," she whispered. Her lips stiffened so that she could scarcely speak. "I can't bear this house a moment longer." He only stared at her. "Richard!" she said pleadingly, afraid of the silence.

"But I want to stay." He caught her wrist and held it very tightly. "I have something to say to you."

"Say it outside. You know I will listen to you."

"This place is better. No one can hear us. We are out of the rain, and alone."

"Are you ill?"

"No, I'm not ill."

"What is it that you want to say? You are hurting my arm."

"How can I tell you when you are angry?" He loosened his grip of her wrist, stared at the marks he had made there, tried to stroke them away.

"I killed a girl," he said casually.

She began to walk down the stairs again, a little in front of him, her legs heavy as if she were walking in a nightmare, loud seas pounding in her ears.

"Why are you afraid?" he asked.

Looking down into the dark hall, she said: "I'm not afraid."

He took her by the shoulders. "I wouldn't hurt you."

"Of course not."

"All you have to do is listen."

"Tell me then."

"From the beginning cruelty always frightened me but I liked frightening myself, and other people. If dogs cowered when I hit them, I hit them all the more. When I was a child, I had to take a much younger child to school. I used to set off from the house, very mealy-mouthed to his mother, and then one day I began to run on ahead. I knew it was wrong. I knew I should always remember it with disgust. It sickened me at the time to look back and see his terror, his fat little legs trying to run, his face red, his mouth open, blubbering. But I couldn't stop. The more I was disgusted, the faster I ran, on and on, only slowing down so that I could keep him in sight and enjoy his terror. It gave me a strange feeling of excitement and tension. I was always bored as a child and lonely. A dull home, a dull provincial town, Sunday walks in my best clothes, stuffed and uncomfortable, watching my reflection going along in shop blinds; Chapel, Sunday-school. I used to sit on the edge of my bed and feel a dreadful kind of power rushing up through my body. Only bouts of cruelty quietened me. I liked frightening people, liked frightening myself. But nothing went deep enough to quieten me for long. There seemed to be hours and hours of sitting there on my bed, wondering what to do next."

He put his hand on her throat, touched the throbbing pulse with his fingers. She tried to speak, but the words seemed too heavy to utter.

"Love was nothing," he said, and kissed her mouth. They stared at one another. "Nothing touched me.

Making love exasperated me. Every depravity angered me. I was cruel to that girl. She had frightened little ways, and I frightened her till she died."

"You couldn't have done that," she whispered.

"No. I strangled her."

"What had she done to you?"

"Nothing. But she bored me, irritated me. I thought death would be more interesting perhaps than love. I thought it might finish something that love never finished. And the excitement of outwitting other people . . ."

"Are you sorry now?"

"It isn't real. She wasn't real to me and now I've forgotten. I didn't even remember her name until I read it afterwards in newspapers." He touched his pocket, hesitated, and then put his hand back on the banisters, very close to hers.

"At first when I came here, I was in high spirits. I felt excited and tense. Then the loneliness began again. That frowsty hotel bedroom. The time dragged. And then I started to lose my nerve. I began to know that I hadn't been so clever, that the police know things sometimes and keep quiet about them. For a long time. No, don't interrupt me. You didn't guess all this about me, did you?"

She shut her eyes. "No, not all this." She thought: 'But cruelty goes from strength to strength. I ought to have feared him more than I did.'

"You don't know anything about me."

"No."

"People like me don't come into your life."

She moved her head.

"But you thought it might be interesting to have a change . . ."

"There was no choice. There were no others . . ." She moved angrily, as if she would wrest herself away from him, but he caught her arm again.

"What are you going to do?" she asked.

"I told you that I'm going away."

"Another hotel bedroom. And so on for the rest of your life."

"I have a dislike of being watched. There are probably others with that man. When he is ready, at a glance from him, they'll close in, without any warning. At present it is all a dream. But suppose it suddenly became real, suppose I woke up in a cell one morning and heard a voice in my mind saying: 'This is real. At last it is real.' Would you wish that for me?"

"Not for anyone."

"Some women like to be treated cruelly. . . ."

Stepping after him from one irrelevancy to another, she tried to follow the direction of his thoughts, to make out his intention. "So I have heard," she said.

"But I wouldn't harm you. I wrote in my diary that I would never touch you in any way but kindness. . . ."

She tried not to glance down at her wrist, so tightly screwed in his fingers that she felt it was on fire. 'If ever I get out of here,' she thought, 'I am entangled in this horror for the rest of my life.'

"You are thinking I am hurting you *now*," he said slyly.

249

'*He* is the sort of person,' she thought again and again. The other world, the world of violence, of people in newspapers, crept round about her, a world she had scarcely believed in. Parting the leaves to look for treasure, love, adventure, she inadvertently disclosed evil, and recoiled. 'He is like this empty, cobwebbed house,' she thought. 'Room after room is full of echoes, there's nothing there.'

"I've listened," she said. "Now can we go?"

"It's still raining."

"It doesn't matter."

"You minded the rain before. Now it is nothing."

"I think you are ill. You are shivering."

"We could find some wood, perhaps, and light a fire in one of the rooms and dry our clothes."

"Someone would see the smoke . . ."

"There is no one to see."

"There are plenty to see. Cottages not a hundred yards away."

"Don't lie to me."

She made no answer.

"I absolutely rely on you to see me through this . . . to keep me company."

"But it's getting late. . . . You will draw attention to yourself by going back . . ."

"I may not go back. For God's sake don't be artful with me. Perhaps you think I'm going to strangle *you*."

"The idea had occurred to me."

"I told you I wouldn't hurt you."

"Yes, over and over again."

She tried to raise her arm and he unclasped her wrist. The white marks of his fingers slowly reddened.

"Go, if you want to," he said indifferently. He suddenly knew that she was no use to him.

He handed her a cigarette and lit it; stared at the match until it went out. She was afraid to move.

"Why don't you go?"

He sat down on the bottom stair and rested his forehead on the palms of his hands. Quite disillusioned now; he knew that she would never support him in his fear. She was herself afraid.

She moved a little way across the hall.

"The rain has stopped," she said, her eyes never leaving him.

"Don't edge your way out like that, and think you are covering it with conversation. I'm not a lunatic. Just go."

"I don't know how to."

He moved his forehead wearily in his hands.

"Goodbye, then," she said.

He didn't answer, and his eyes were closed.

She was afraid to turn her back to him, felt imaginary hands grasping her ankles as she began to move. At the kitchen door, terror hastened her. A mouse ran across the threshold. Outside, the drenched garden seemed bowed down under its great weight of water, the leaves dripped steadily. She slipped on the mossy path and twisted her ankle. Then she began to run, limping with the pain. She ran for a long time, until

251

her shoulders ached and each breath seemed to be torn out of her lungs.

While she was running, she could not think, but as soon as she began to walk, words sorted themselves out in her mind. She took her damp handkerchief from her pocket to wipe her face, and a piece of paper dropped on to the gravelly road. She could scarcely bend from the stitch in her side, but she stooped and picked it up. It was the cheque she had written earlier in the evening. It was wet now and the ink smudged. She had sat at the dressing-table writing it, and Liz had come in to feed the baby. It was days ago, and a different world. "Only remember that I love you," Liz had said or some words like those. "I love you. I wish you to be happy."

With the crushed-up paper in her hand, she began to run again. At the Hand and Flowers the door was shut, but the curtains in the bar were not drawn. She could see the stuffed fish on the wall, the landlord collecting the glasses.

Morland was on his way home. He was walking along singing to himself, and as he turned the corner she ran into his arms.

. . . . .

The station was empty. A few lights, yellow and emerald, were reflected in the black, wet platform. Rain dripped still from the spiked shelter.

Richard walked through the entrance, past the railings with the familiar advertisements; the blot of ink, enamelled on tin; Wincarnis, Ovaltine.

'I am going to Scarborough,' he told himself.

His shirt was dirty. He had no luggage. Cobweb clung to his sleeve. 'I am going up North,' he thought. Each time he said this, the jazzy little room receded from his mind, together with his father's voice, his mother's look, home, reality. Instead, the wind blew in from the sea, across the asphalt spaces, barbed wire was looped against the invader, screens across pub doors hung between the light and the street.

His steps made a hollow clangour on the footbridge. He tried to walk more quietly, tiptoed up the greasy stairs. Sooty raindrops gathered and fell from the wooden canopy; below, the lines curved away, out into the country, past the earthworks set on the hill, past the backs of houses, black canals, little fields; the English landscape.

The express came down on the middle line, casting away its smoke, to left and right, hastening through this unimportant little station, going north.

As it screamed towards him, he grasped the wet iron ledge with both hands and hoisted himself up.

THE END

IN PRAISE OF ELIZABETH TAYLOR

'She is sophisticated, sensitive and brilliantly amusing, with a kind of stripped, piercing feminine wit and a power of creating and maintaining a fine nervous tension' – *Rosamond Lehmann*

'Like Jane Austen, like Barbara Pym, like Elizabeth Bowen – soul sisters all – Elizabeth Taylor made it her business to explore the quirky underside of so-called civilization' – *Anne Tyler*

'One of our foremost novelists' – *Angus Wilson*

At Mrs Lippincote's: 'A book for the epicure, who will delight in its deftness, its compression, its under- and over-tones' – *L. P. Hartley*

The Blush: 'Here Mrs Taylor displays her gifts – her quite extraordinary gift – for sheer situation – not a tale here fails to expand in the imagination of the reader' – *Elizabeth Bowen*

THE NOVELS OF ELIZABETH TAYLOR

Also of interest from Virago

THE NOVELS OF NINA BAWDEN

THE BIRDS ON THE TREES

'Nina Bawden gets inside the skins of all her people and shows them as paradoxical, crotchety, adulterous, ambitious and completely human . . . A beautifully sustained impression of the impossibility of family life' – *New York Times Book Review*

FAMILY MONEY

'Nina Bawden's marvellous new novel . . . funny, subtle, sympathetic' – *Observer*

THE GRAIN OF TRUTH

'This is the off-side of lust in plush suburbia, described by a crypto-moralist with a mischievous sense of humour'
– *Sunday Times*

THE ICE HOUSE

'Nina Bawden's talent is to be able to take you along a perfectly ordinary street, rip the façade away and show the strange and passionate events that go on behind closed doors'
– *Daily Telegraph*

A LITTLE LOVE, A LITTLE LEARNING

'Nina Bawden writes with enormous subtlety and understanding here about the pains and joys of growing up. On every page there is a shock of recognition' – *Sunday Telegraph*

TORTOISE BY CANDLELIGHT

'An exceptional picture of disorganised family life . . . Imaginative, tender, with a welcome undercurrent of toughness' – *Observer*

WALKING NAKED

'Dazzlingly effective . . . not easy to forget' – *Financial Times*

A WOMAN OF MY AGE

'Rarely have the workings of a woman's mind been revealed with such clarity' – *Daily Telegraph*

THE NOVELS OF REBECCA WEST

'Reviewing Rebecca West is like trying to review Michelangelo. Perhaps we have become afraid of acknowledging contemporary greatness' – *Sybille Bedford*

'Rebecca West – highly intelligent, highly gifted, vital, original, combative, formidable and kind – was a great woman'
– *Victoria Glendinning*

'One must conclude tha the greatest living example of a woman . . . who has been both thinker and an artist, and who has managed over some sixty years to express a spacious sense of reality , is Rebecca West' – *Samuel Hynes, The Times Literary Supplement*

THE FOUNTAIN OVERFLOWS

THIS REAL NIGHT

THE BIRDS FALL DOWN

COUSIN ROSAMUND

HARRIET HUME

THE HARSH VOICE

THE JUDGE

THE RETURN OF THE SOLDIER

SUNFLOWER

THE THINKING REED